PROCEED TO
JUDGEMENT

PROCEED TO JUDGEMENT

Sara Woods

I charge you by the law,
Whereof you are a well-deserving pillar,
Proceed to judgement.

> *Merchant of Venice*, Act IV, scene i

St. Martin's Press
New York

Library of Congress Cataloging in Publication Data

Woods, Sara, pseud.
  Proceed to judgement.

  I. Title.
PZ4.W895Pr 1980   [PR6073.063]   823'.9'14   79-22854
ISBN 0-312-64776-X

Any work of fiction whose characters were of uniform excellence
would rightly be condemned – by that fact if by no other – as
being incredibly dull. Therefore no excuse can be considered
necessary for the villainy or folly of the people appearing in this
book. It seems extremely unlikely that any one of them should
resemble a real person, alive or dead. Any such resemblance is
completely unintentional and without malice.

                                                              S.W.

PART ONE

MICHAELMAS TERM, 1971

MONDAY 15th NOVEMBER

I

'This is a very unorthodox approach,' said Kevin O'Brien comfortably. He was stretched out at his ease in one of the wing chairs in the Maitlands' living-room, and the statement, if it was true, didn't seem to be causing him any anxiety. 'But you, of all men,' he added, 'won't be disturbed by that.'

Antony Maitland, who was standing on the hearthrug, a little to one side of the fire, exchanged a brief, resigned look with his wife. Jenny had taken her favourite place, and looked as relaxed as O'Brien did, curled up in one corner of the sofa; she was quite prepared to remain a listener only, withdrawn from the conversation, but she recognised the mood that prompted the exchange of glances. Her husband's attention was caught, but there was also a little uneasiness. Because there had been so many discussions, some of them in this very room, that had started in just that way, and if she were to start trying to remember where all of them had led . . .

But that was an unprofitable train of thought. She turned instead to a contemplation of their visitor, whom she had met on a number of occasions without knowing well. O'Brien was a tall, narrow-shouldered man with a hint of austerity in his look; but when he smiled all that was forgotten, and people generally did smile at Jenny. Even in ordinary conversation there was a richness about his voice. Antony could have told her that in court it could be very impressive indeed.

Maitland had murmured something in response to that first experimental remark, something non-committal that brought a rather sardonic look to O'Brien's face. 'You're

7

wondering why I should be disturbing your evening,' he said, 'and it's puzzled I am myself, you see, just how best to explain it.' The hint of brogue that occasionally coloured his voice was, Maitland knew, completely spurious, O'Brien having been born and brought up in Yorkshire. There had been a time when this would have exasperated him, but he knew his fellow barrister better now. As much – he caught himself up rather ruefully on the thought – as anyone could expect to know that rather enigmatic man.

'I suppose,' he said, and if the words were tentative it was because he knew them to be trite, 'it's something about a case.'

'It is that.'

'One that you haven't time to take on yourself, perhaps?' That was nonsense, and he knew it. The solicitor concerned would have been in touch with Mallory by now, no need for O'Brien's intervention; especially as he seemed unexpectedly, and certainly uncharacteristically, unwilling to come to the point.

'Not exactly,' Kevin said now. 'A brief I have accepted. But there are two defendants.'

'And two sets of solicitors who can't agree – ' Maitland began, but broke off there as he realised that this explanation didn't make much sense either. 'You'd better begin at the beginning,' he said, resigned, and picked up his brandy snifter from where he had placed it by the clock and went to seat himself in the chair opposite the one O'Brien had taken. If there was a story to be told he would have preferred to be at liberty to roam about the room at will while it was in the telling, but perhaps the other man would speak more freely if his audience were at rest.

'Very well.' Kevin sipped his cognac, replaced the glass on the table at his elbow, and gave Jenny an apologetic look. 'If I bore you, Mrs Maitland, I must ask your forgiveness in advance.'

'I shan't be bored,' said Jenny. She had already offered to

retire when it became obvious that this was to be to some degree a professional conference, and she didn't bother to repeat the suggestion. 'But you're beginning to alarm me,' she added.

O'Brien had a puzzled look for that, followed almost immediately by one of comprehension. 'You're thinking I want to involve him in something dangerous,' he said, and gave her one of his most persuasive smiles. 'Now, would I be doing a thing like that?' His glance at Antony conveyed clearly enough that had they been alone together he would have reminded him that any such involvement in the past had been at Maitland's instigation, not his. 'No, no, this is quite a simple little matter, no complications at all.'

Jenny smiled back at him. She might have believed him, or she might have been reserving judgement. 'If you don't want us both to die of curiosity, Mr O'Brien – ' she said.

'Very well,' said Kevin again, but in spite of this his eyes lingered for a moment on her face. Antony, for one, thought this reasonable enough. Without being a beauty, Jenny was undeniably good to look upon. She had brown-gold hair that curled closely about her head with no regard for the fashion of the day, a short, straight nose, and rather wide-set grey eyes that gave her a look of candour. On the whole that was a fair impression, though her husband could have quoted you times when she had used this gift of nature with deliberate intent to deceive. Now he watched patiently while O'Brien took stock of these attributes, and wondered if Jenny was really reassured by the protestation of normality. For himself, he liked the other man well enough, and was inclined to think he would like him better the more he knew of him. But all that was without prejudice to the knowledge that he could be a crafty devil when he wanted to be.

At last O'Brien seemed to have finished his inspection. 'You'll have heard,' he said, turning a little to divide the remark between them, 'of the Johnstone murder.'

'One could hardly help it.' Maitland's tone was dry. 'Not

that the newspapers give you a very good picture.' He paused, contemplating it, and then shook his head, perhaps over the meagreness of the information at his disposal. 'All I really know is that they seem very excited about it.'

'Well, come now,' O'Brien wasn't going to let him get away with quite such a protestation of ignorance. 'You've heard of Johnstone and Lamb. Everybody has.'

'Except me,' said Jenny. 'Who are they?'

'Stockbrokers.'

'Then I don't quite see why everybody –'

'They have flair,' said O'Brien simply. 'They make money, even their clients make money . . . but that's really nothing to do with the case.'

'A rather sordid, domestic killing,' said Maitland didactically. 'Which one of the defendants are you representing?'

'Mrs Johnstone.'

'And the other chap, the doctor who is said to have been her lover.' Maitland seemed to have forgotten that he had professed to be unfamiliar with the matter. 'I should have said myself that it was a case for a joint defence, but if his solicitor has other ideas – '

'It isn't as simple as that.'

'Tell me, then!'

'Mrs Johnstone started life as Kate Harley. They're an old family, landed people who have somehow managed to hold on to a reasonable amount of their cash. They have a country place, I think, not very grand but they seem to have always lived mainly in town. Their solicitor is a chap called David Shaw. I don't know if you know him.'

'Shaw, Davidson and Cooper? I've heard of them.'

'Not your line of country. Shaw is completely out of his depth in a matter like this, of course, but he had at least sufficient sense,' said Kevin, grinning, 'to brief me on his client's behalf. That's where things started to get interesting. The other solicitor, Collingwood's, wanted to make common cause of the matter, but the Harleys won't have that at any price.'

'I don't quite see – '

'Their tale is, you see, that Kate acted under Collingwood's influence. They want me to exonerate her, in so far as that can be done without denying her guilt altogether, by throwing the greater part of the blame on him.'

'Well, it is a point of view, of course.'

'And as they're footing the bill – '

'I can see the difficulty. But where do you come in. O'Brien? Unless you think I'd make so inept an adversary . . . and even then I should have thought it was up to this Dr Collingwood's solicitor to approach me.'

Kevin closed his eyes for a moment, and when he opened them again the look he gave Antony was half rueful, half amused. 'A chap in our profession should be able to express himself better than that, shouldn't he? We'll try again. For my own reasons, which I'll come to in a moment, I want Collingwood to have the best representation – '

'I'm flattered, of course, but – '

' – but in this case it was obvious what result an approach to you through Mallory would have. He'd have turned it down flat.'

Maitland had a frown for that. 'Why?' he asked.

'His notions on the subject of fees are notorious.'

'Mr Mallory is very . . . devoted,' said Jenny.

Antony, surprised perhaps by the interruption and still more by this description of Sir Nicholas Harding's clerk, who was anything but devoted to his employer's nephew, glanced in her direction and saw that her eyes were dancing. What he had called a sordid, domestic matter might be dull, but at least it held no terrors for her. His frown was banished, and when O'Brien added, 'Collingwood hasn't a bean,' the bland simplicity of the statement brought a reluctant smile to Maitland's lips. 'I'd offer to share my fee with you,'

11

said Kevin handsomely, 'only I do think there's some doubt whether I'll ever collect it.'

'That seems to be another statement that needs some explanation.'

'I told you the Harleys had their own ideas as to how the defence should be conducted. When I explain to them that I've no intention of complying with their wishes . . . I'll have the brief marked a guinea if I have to,' said O'Brien pugnaciously, 'but I'm not giving it up.'

'Douglas Johnstone's estate? No, of course, if your client is convicted she'll have no claim. But if you intend to quarrel with her parents anyway there seems no reason why you can't conduct both defences yourself.'

Kevin looked at him for a long moment. 'You're being very obtuse about this, Maitland,' he said at last, and annoyingly reached for his cognac and began to sip it slowly without attempting to enlighten his companions further. Jenny, watching her husband's expression, laughed aloud.

'Don't you see, Antony,' she said, 'Mr O'Brien thinks both the accused people are innocent?'

'That has been becoming increasingly obvious. All the same . . . why me?'

'Because he wants to know the truth. You've said yourself often enough it's the only real defence. And you've had a lot of experience – more than most people – in ferreting out the real facts of a case.'

The humorous look about Maitland's eyes was very marked now. 'I could think of more attractive ways of putting it,' he said thoughtfully, and in his turn made something of a ceremony of taking a little brandy. '*Is* that what you meant, O'Brien?' he demanded, when the glass was safely back on the table again.

'It's exactly what I mean,' said Kevin, so enthusiastically that it seemed he must have been holding himself in check while Jenny was speaking.

'And what makes you think I'll take it on?'

12

'That's more difficult. There's a phrase that I've heard bandied about – I don't know who started it – about your activities. "He's off on one of his damned crusades". So I thought perhaps –'

'I see.' There was cause for amusement here too, if only the other man could see it, because if ever there was a champion of lost causes, who flung himself into every new battle with unbridled enthusiasm, it was Kevin O'Brien, Q.C. 'What little I've read about this matter doesn't exactly convince me . . . of course, you know more about it than I do,' Antony added politely. 'But, you see, the thing about my "damned crusades", as you call them, is that they're usually undertaken on behalf of people I believe to be innocent. And you could be wrong about that,' he pointed out apologetically.

O'Brien knew him at least well enough to take the apology with a grain of salt, and said cheerfully, 'I'm not.'

'I've only your word for that.'

Kevin, who affected at times a sleepy look, opened his eyes wide at that. 'Are you calling my judgement into question, my dear fellow?' he asked. Jenny, resisting the temptation to say, 'Antony only meant –' got up and fetched the brandy decanter. 'Because if you are –' said O'Brien, and broke off as she reached his side.

'I think you'd better tell me,' said Antony, not looking at their guest now, but watching his wife's ministrations, 'what Mrs Johnstone's position is in all this.'

'She says she didn't do it. Well, I admit,' said Kevin, making the admission glibly, 'I didn't altogether believe her at first. But there's something about her, you'll see what I mean when you see her for yourself, I suppose you'd call it a sincerity.'

'I gather she's a good-looking woman,' said Maitland unkindly.

'As a matter of fact, she is . . . very. Well, but look,' – he was very much in earnest – 'that has absolutely nothing to

13

do with it. I think I can tell by now when a witness is telling the truth.'

But that was the trouble with O'Brien; give him a cause that he could persuade himself was a good one and there was no holding him. Maitland, himself often a prey to doubt, had frequently had occasion to envy the other man his certainties. In the present case, however . . .

'*Was* this Dr Collingwood her lover?' he asked abruptly. It was at least an alternative to conveying his misgivings to O'Brien, which would not be a popular move, however tactfully it might be done.

'She doesn't admit it, only that she's very, very fond of him.' Kevin, it seemed, was quite capable of laughing at his own foibles, and Maitland relaxed a little.

'Do you believe that too?' he asked lightly.

'Now, that's a thing I'm not sure about. She's very positive, however, that he had nothing to do with her husband's death.'

'Have you seen Collingwood?'

'I have.'

'How did he impress you?'

'Well, on the whole. There's no doubt he's in love with the woman, but, as I see it, if she's innocent, so is he.'

Maitland came to his feet and took a quick turn to the window and back to the hearth again. This time he did not seat himself. 'You'd better tell me something of the circumstances,' he said, capitulating.

O'Brien did not seem particularly elated by the invitation. 'Douglas Johnstone was a man in his forties,' he said, and gave the appearance of choosing his words carefully. 'He was a diabetic, needing regular injections of insulin, which he generally gave himself. Somebody substituted an overdose of morphine, and there he was . . . dead.'

Antony showed his teeth in a singularly mirthless grin. 'That leaves a hundred questions unanswered,' he pointed out.

14

'I'm well aware of it. I seem to have heard, however, that you have a weakness for getting your facts at first hand.'

'There's something to be said for it,' Maitland agreed. 'Roughly, though, what is the prosecution's case?'

'Quarrels. There's some evidence she wanted a divorce, and he said he'd never give up the children. She wanted an amicable parting, he said he could prove adultery, and in the circumstances there's no question who would have got custody.'

'Well, that's motive . . . and very nice too. What about the rest of it?'

'Opportunity? The syringe was left in Johnstone's bathroom, it was his habit to refill it after each injection. And you know in those circumstances – '

'Servants?' asked Mailand abruptly, and went back to the window again.

'No earthly reason for any of them to have done such a thing. Nobody seems to have been under notice, and he wasn't the sort of man, from all I can make out, to have been dishing out legacies right and left. Besides, there's more.'

Maitland turned from his contemplation of the square below. 'I thought there might be,' he said.

'Dr Collingwood called on Mrs Johnstone early in the afternoon. Later she was seen coming out of her husband's room. The maid who saw her was surprised, they hadn't been sleeping together for some time. And there is a certain amount of morphine missing from the practice Collingwood belongs to; he's employed by a Dr John Trevelyan, who incidentally numbers both the Harleys and the Johnstones among his patients.'

Antony ignored that. He came back to the fire again, this time more slowly; a tall, dark man with more sensitivity than was perhaps good for him. More of a sense of humour, too, though at the moment he was wholly serious. He was moving rather stiffly, and Jenny, watching him, thought,

15

'He's interested, too interested to remember that his shoulder has been hurting him lately. This case may be just what he needs, difficult enough to keep him occupied without the danger of that affair last month.' But Maitland was looking at the visitor in rather a sombre way.

'Explanations?' he said.

'You won't like them,' Kevin warned, and this time Antony smiled.

'I don't expect I shall,' he said. 'You'd hardly be making all this fuss – '

'All right!' Perhaps purposefully, the words sounded like a threat. 'Collingwood told the police he called because the little boy, Dougie, had a cold. Not very sensible of him when the other doctor, his employer, had been to the house to see the patient only that morning, and was the Johnstones' regular physician as well. When this was pointed out to Collingwood he just said it was his own business, nothing to do with any one else.'

'And this is the chap you're wishing on me as a client! Was yours any more co-operative?'

'Only up to a point. She said it was a social call to ask about Dougie, nothing out of the way from a friend of the family.'

'Was the child so desperately ill?'

'A bad case of the sniffles, no more, according to Dr Trevelyan. I told you – ' he added, seeing Maitland's expression, but did not attempt to complete the thought.

'So you did. And you're quite right, I don't like it at all. But let's take my emotions for granted, shall we, and get on to these explanations of yours? Why was Mrs Johnstone, against all precedent, coming from her husband's room?'

'She says her maid, who looks after small repairs to her husband's wardrobe too, had been growing careless, and she wanted to check that all his shirts had buttons on. It *could* be true,' said O'Brien, this time sounding extremely sceptical. 'She said it was a sort of partisanship on the maid's part, and

16

she didn't see why Douglas should suffer because of the woman's attitude.'

'Didn't Johnstone have his own manservant?'

'No.'

'In view of his financial position – '

'I gather,' said Kevin, very solemnly, 'that in some way it was against his religion.' He watched the effect of that on his audience for a moment, and then added with a touch of impatience in his voice, 'I don't understand these puritans.'

'Is that what he is? I don't understand them myself, for that matter,' added Maitland thoughtfully. 'Was he a religious man?'

'No particular religion, as far as I've been able to make out. Just a general conviction that anything pleasant must be sinful.'

Maitland grimaced. 'Perhaps you could get away with a plea of justifiable homicide,' he suggested. 'Seriously though, I gather their marital differences were common knowledge in the household.'

'The trouble between them was of very long standing.'

'The maid took her mistress's part. What about the rest of the staff?'

'They were Johnstone's servants, already in his employment when he married ten years ago. They were ready enough to give evidence of the ill-feeling between husband and wife.'

'I see.' Maitland thought about that for a moment. 'You do realise – don't you? – that every answer you give me opens up a whole new series of questions.'

'All the more reason,' said O'Brien at his blandest, 'why you should see these people for yourself.'

'Wait a bit! There's still the most important question of all. What about this missing morphine?'

'A certain amount of spillage, I think they call it, is expected. Collingwood says so, at any rate, and it seems Trevelyan agrees with him.'

'You're telling me nothing could be proved either way.'

'That's about it. Look here, Maitland, won't you see Collingwood at least?'

'What's the position there?'

'His solicitor is a personal friend of his, a chap called Kells. I don't have to tell you there are any number of up-and-coming youngsters who'd jump at the chance of the brief, in view of the fact that the matter seems to have caught the public fancy. Yes,' he added, rather hurriedly, 'I know that's a strike against it from your point of view, but Collingwood needs the sort of help you can give him. For that matter,' he admitted ingenuously, so that Antony smiled again, and this time with real amusement, 'so does my client. So I persuaded Kells to hold off on any decision until I'd seen you.'

'I'm not surprised you started out with an apology for unorthodox behaviour.'

'It wasn't so much an apology,' O'Brien pointed out, 'as a statement of fact.'

'So it was. The idea then is that Kells should approach Mallory, whom I have in the meantime instructed to accept the brief for a nominal fee.' He glanced at Jenny, and saw that she was as alive as he was to the humour of the situation. 'Yes, love, it can be done, but at what cost? But you see what this means, don't you, O'Brien? I'm committed to take Collingwood on as a client before I've ever seen him.'

'Is that so unusual?'

'Of course it isn't. But in view of what you're asking me, which is to conduct an investigation . . . I won't do it unless I've a pretty good idea there's something to uncover.'

'That's fair enough.' O'Brien turned his attention to his cognac again, but after a moment he too turned to Jenny. 'I don't mind telling you, Mrs Maitland, investigation or no investigation, there's no one I'd rather have as a colleague in this difficult case.'

18

II

'Not that it should be so *very* difficult,' said Jenny later, after O'Brien had gone. 'I think I'm glad you said you'd take it on.'

'Therapy?' said Antony, smiling at her.

'What I meant – '

'I know what you meant, exactly, love. Something interesting enough to keep me fully occupied, so that there's not much chance ... I'm sorry about that affair last month, Jenny, really I am.'

'Well you must admit it sounds like a nice change,' said Jenny, ignoring the apology.

'If Mallory doesn't murder me himself when I break it to him.' But Jenny wasn't rising to that one either, she only smiled at him sedately. 'I'm curious,' he admitted, when it became obvious she wasn't going to respond, 'to meet this couple whom O'Brien seems ready to take on trust.'

'I always thought, if his sympathies were engaged – '

'That's the snag, of course, he's an emotional chap.'

'While you, of course, are ruled entirely by intellect.'

'More so than he is, anyway,' insisted her husband stubbornly. He picked up a couple of the brandy glasses and made for the door. 'And if you're going to resort to irony, my love,' he said over his shoulder, 'it's high time we went to bed.'

TUESDAY, 16th NOVEMBER

I

The interview with Mr Mallory, who was old and set in his ways, was no easier than he had expected. At best, the clerk tolerated the younger members of Sir Nicholas's chambers; at worst, which was where Maitland came in, he positively disapproved of them. Of course, there could be no question that Antony would eventually get his own way, but the process could be wearing.

The relationship between Antony Maitland and his uncle, Sir Nicholas Harding, was a closer one than that which ordinarily exists between uncle and nephew. Antony had joined the bachelor establishment in Kempenfeldt Square upon the death of his father when he was only a few days past his thirteenth birthday; and later, when housing was scarce, the tall old house had been divided to provide married quarters for himself and Jenny on the two top floors. If all three of the people concerned were telling the truth, the arrangement had been meant to be a temporary one, but somehow it had continued through the years. There had seemed some promise of change when Sir Nicholas, acting impulsively for perhaps the first time in his life, had married at the end of the previous Trinity Term, Miss Vera Langhorne, barrister-at-law; but now that the long vacation was over and the Michaelmas term well launched, the household seemed to have expanded comfortably to include the new Lady Harding.

In addition, Maitland had been, since he came out of his pupilage, a member of Sir Nicholas's chambers in the Inner Temple. There were times when he would have said it was a disadvantage to live under the same roof as well, when his uncle wished to speak his mind with his customary freedom about some one or other of the younger man's activities. On the other hand, there were undoubted advantages in fighting one's battles on one's own ground.

But this morning the battle was with Mallory, and much less invigorating than an engagement with Sir Nicholas would have been. 'I can't possibly be free before five o'clock,' Antony said at last with finality, 'but if Mr Kells doesn't mind putting in a little overtime we might go down to Brixton together then.' Mallory went away with a dissatisfied look, and delayed bringing the return message of agreement with this arrangement until nearly three o'clock in the afternoon, so that Antony – who ought to have known better – felt guilty when he phoned Jenny to advise her that he would be late. 'Never mind,' she told him cheerfully, 'I shall have Vera and Uncle Nick to keep me company.' That was one of the traditions, that Sir Nicholas should dine with them on Tuesday evenings when his housekeeper, Mrs Stokes, was out. Jenny suspected that Vera would have been glad enough to have the run of the kitchen for an evening, but though, to everyone's surprise, she had the two permanent members of her household staff eating out of her hand, that would almost certainly have proved too much for them to swallow.

Richard Kells arrived in chambers at about ten to five and Willett, one of the junior clerks who for one reason and another considered Maitland's affairs particularly his own preserve, brought him along to the narrow, rather dark room where Antony worked. Antony, who was sorting through a tangle of papers in a rather despairing way, said thankfully, 'Can I leave these to you, Willett?' and turned to survey the solicitor with an interest that he soon saw, with amusement, was being returned.

Kells was thirtyish, and looked more like a professional rugger player than a lawyer, though he was correctly enough attired for a business day. Maitland, who had risen, estimated that the newcomer topped his own height by at least two inches; his hair was darkish and waved strongly, but meeting his eyes, which were brown and rather deepset, Antony decided that there was no lack of intelligence there. He said abruptly, because the other man's frank appraisal suddenly made him uneasy, 'Did you really want me, or did O'Brien do a con job on you too?' He thought he heard Willett, busy among the papers on the desk, click his tongue reprovingly but his attention was all for the man he was addressing.

If Kells was startled by this somewhat original form of greeting, he didn't show it. He said instead, lightly, 'The opportunity of briefing someone as . . . celebrated . . . as yourself doesn't come every day. In the circumstances I must thank you for taking the matter on, and Mr O'Brien, I suppose, for persuading you to do so.'

It was touch and go whether Maitland lost his temper at that; he didn't like any reminder of the publicity that had sometimes attended his affairs. As it was he remarked, equally lightly, 'O'Brien is an eloquent man.' And then, with a touch of embarrassment which was uncharacteristic where professional matters were concerned, 'I don't know how frankly you have spoken together on the subject.'

Willett said, 'I'll finish these later, Mr Maitland,' and went out, closing the door firmly behind him. Antony waved a hand in vague invitation and sank back into the chair behind the desk again, but his eyes never left the visitor's face as the solicitor too seated himself.

'I think I may say there was some pretty plain speaking,' said Richard Kells. There was a trace of amusement in his voice, but some curiosity as well. Maitland chose to satisfy that with a little more outspokenness.

'What I'm getting at: I've taken the brief. Whatever I feel when I've seen our client, I shall study it diligently and do the best with the facts you give me in court. But O'Brien wants more than that, he's quite convinced of both his and our clients' innocence. I've told him straight, as I'm telling you now, I won't get mixed up in an investigation unless I'm convinced there are reasonable grounds for doubt.'

'I think I'm fairly clear about that.' There was still the appraising look. 'But "reasonable grounds" covers an awful lot of territory, Mr Maitland.'

'So it does.' And I'm talking to you to avoid the moment of going out to the prison, of realising fully, as I shall be forced to do, that here is a man who can't get out, against whom the doors are locked and barred. And inevitably I shall agree to what all these people want – even Jenny – because it would be intolerable to make a false judgement. And perhaps I shall be right, and perhaps I shall be wrong; either way, the doubts will follow. And perhaps this chap here understands something of all this, I wouldn't put it past him. 'What do you know of Dr Collingwood?' he demanded.

For the first time the solicitor seemed a little taken aback. 'He's a friend of mine,' he said cautiously.

'Then first you can expand on that. How long have you known him?'

'We both came from the same town. Tilham, in Sussex. Do you know it?'

'I was born there.' He didn't wait for Kells to exclaim over the coincidence. 'But I left for good when I was thirteen years old. Before your time.'

'Yes, well, the funny thing was James and I didn't know each other until we went away to school. But then I suppose coming from the same place brought us together. Anyway, that's how it was. Of course, we didn't see so much of each other after we left, because I did my articles in Tilham, and he got a scholarship to a medical school in the north. But we kept in touch, and found ourselves living quite close together again when he joined Dr Trevelyan.'

'You realise I don't even know yet where all these dire events took place.'

'No, I suppose you don't. Do you know Wilgrave Square?' Maitland nodded. 'Both the Harleys and the Johnstones live

23

there . . . the Douglas Johnstones, I mean. Dr Trevelyan is just round the corner from them, in Cheston Place, while I'm in digs much nearer Victoria Station.'

'And Dr Collingwood?'

'Didn't I make that clear? He lives with the Trevelyans. Which explains, really, how he came to know Kate. And there's something else I should explain to you –'

'If you're going to talk about money . . . don't!'

'In fairness to James,' said Kells doggedly. Not a man, evidently, to be easily turned from his purpose. 'I don't think his family ever had much money really, not as the Harleys and the Johnstones of this world regard it, anyway. His father was a building contractor and wasn't in any difficulty about school fees, or about helping out a bit when James was in medical school. But his death, just about the time James graduated, happened to coincide with a slump in the industry. There was just enough to buy a tiny annuity for Mrs Collingwood. James has been helping her out ever since, and of course there's been no question of his buying into a practice.'

'I see.' Maitland sounded thoughtful. 'What does he say about . . . about the charge, for instance?'

'I thought you understood that the plea will be Not Guilty.'

'There's still no harm in telling me –'

'He didn't supply the morphine. The amount the police claim is missing is no more than can be ordinarily accounted for.' Kells hesitated. 'That's what he says. I think he's a little uneasy about it, though.'

'What has Dr Trevelyan to say to that, I wonder.'

'He'll back James up, but he's uneasy too, and it shows. The thing is, you see, he says he's quite sure no morphine has been administered by him personally to any of his patients . . . you know in that case no record need be kept.'

'I didn't know, but go on.'

'Well, James says the same thing. And the amount of "spil-

24

lage" that is reasonable . . . what's missing, you see, is more than a fatal dose.'

'That's a bit vague. No,' – holding up a hand – 'I don't want any details at the moment, time enough later for all that. But do I take it that you mean, a larger quantity than was administered to Douglas Johnstone . . . whatever that may have been?'

'A considerably larger quantity.'

'Difficult,' said Maitland. He got to his feet as he spoke. 'I'm making you late and I'm sorry,' he added. 'Have you transportation, or shall we look for a cab?'

II

For one reason or another, there was a little delay in producing James Collingwood when they got to the prison. Richard Kells was inclined to be apologetic, as though the whole mix-up had been his fault; but Maitland was too taken up with his own thoughts to pay much heed to that. He disliked this whole business of prison visiting, though in this instance there was obviously no way of avoiding it. But the sooner it was over the better he would be pleased.

Perhaps because of the role the doctor was said to play in the drama that was gradually unfolding, Antony had been expecting something of the order of film-star good looks. When Collingwood at last came in, and the door was closed on them, he proved to be an ordinary enough looking young man, with nothing outstanding about him at first glance but a shock of dark red hair. He was pale, but that was probably natural, nothing to do with his sojourn within these gloomy walls, and though summer was so long behind there were freckles on his face and hands. They were good hands, at once strong and gentle (now, what in the world had put that thought into his head?) and he was a quiet man, who spoke without much gesticulation. Maitland took time to wonder,

25

as the first greetings were exchanged, how deep the veneer of calm really was.

And then they were seated, uncomfortably enough. The long, bare table was dusty, and something had roughened the edge at the end farthest from the door where Maitland had chosen to sit. Some danger of splinters there. He put his elbows firmly on the table, and suppressed his desire to prowl about the room; that must not be done until his client felt so much at ease with him that any rapport that had been built up between them would not be broken. 'From what Richard tells me,' said Collingwood, taking the initiative into his own hands, 'I've some cause to be grateful to you for taking me on.'

That was the last subject Maitland wanted to discuss. 'Let's leave any question of gratitude until the verdict's in,' he suggested, and was relieved when his client, after a quick enquiring glance at his solicitor, had sufficient sensibility to let the matter drop. 'And you may not,' Antony added, with a touch of the humour that was never very far below the surface of his thoughts, 'be so very grateful to me by the time we get going today.'

That seemed to catch the prisoner's interest. 'Why not?' he demanded alertly.

'Because there'll be questions . . . damned impertinent questions you'll think them. This is in the nature of an exploratory session, you know.'

Collingwood considered that, but seemed on the whole inclined to be philosophical. 'No worse than the police questioning, I dare say,' he said. 'And you're on my side.'

'But I have to know – you might as well understand this from the beginning, Doctor – every last thing the prosecution can possibly throw at us in court.'

That brought a touch of colour to the prisoner's cheeks, but he answered steadily enough. 'I think I understand all that.'

'Very well then.' Shoot straight for the heart of the matter, which he generally did instinctively, or work his way in slowly by some innocuous, comparatively unembarrassing route? In the event, Collingwood answered that for him, interrupting his thoughts and asking eagerly, as though he could no longer contain the question.

'Have you seen Kate?'

'Mrs Johnstone? Not yet, though O'Brien is arranging for me to do so. It seemed to me that my first duty was to my own client.'

'Then let me ask you something. As blunt a question as you've promised me. I've heard of you, you see, Mr Maitland . . . "the man who never loses a case". Is it possible that you might get me off and the jury still find Kate guilty?'

'In the first place,' – Maitland, who spent so much of his life asking questions had an incongruous dislike of answering them himself – 'what you've heard is all nonsense. I wish it wasn't, but it is. So I hope you're not relying on any miracles. But as for the rest . . . yes, it is possible, I suppose. I know very little of the matter as yet, you know, so it's hard to say. But anything's possible with a jury.'

'But, you see . . . Richard said – '

'I'm sure Mr Kells told you, O'Brien's as good as they come.' (Collingwood was showing some signs of agitation now.) 'He's a good deal more eloquent than I am, for instance,' Maitland added deliberately.

'It isn't just a matter of eloquence. Don't you see, it's so desperately important – ?' He was still addressing counsel directly, but it was Kells who leaned forward to answer him.

'Mr Maitland has promised Mr O'Brien his co-operation,' he said.

'Yes, I see.' The momentary excitement faded. 'Meanwhile, we're on probation.' There seemed to be no bitterness in his tone, and Antony decided to ignore the remark. The implications, in any event, would have been difficult to answer. Instead he decided to take the plunge *in medias res*, and could tell himself that it was his client's own responsibility for opening the way.

'What is your relationship with Mrs Johnstone?' he asked.

In some way Collingwood seemed to find that the very abruptness of the question had a steadying effect. His hands were still clasped lightly, motionless on the table in front of him. 'I can't answer that except in the tritest way,' he said. 'We were . . . we are . . . good friends.'

'And if you both come out of this unscathed?' He knew as he spoke that was the wrong word to use, for who could escape from their memories? 'Would you still be "good friends", or would the question of marriage arise?'

'How can I say? The situation would be very different, now that Kate is no longer a married woman. I'm trying to be honest with you,' he protested, seeing perhaps some scepticism in Maitland's eye, and suddenly Antony was grinning at him.

'Let's leave your honesty out of it for the time being,' he suggested. 'The thing is, what sort of proof can the prosecution bring that you were lovers?'

He thought Collingwood was going to protest the use of the word, and was inclined to give Kells credit for having been outspoken with his client when the expected objection was not forthcoming. There was again that telltale flush, but the doctor spoke composedly.

'Our only meetings – Richard tells me the police have evidence of this – were in a teashop on the corner of Cheston Place. Hardly the sort of place I'd have chosen with seduction in mind.'

'But you did meet there regularly?'

'Whenever I finished my rounds in time.'

'Mrs Johnstone would be there waiting for you?'

'Well . . . almost every weekday. It was never a long meeting; I wasn't free till late and she liked to get back to have an hour with the children before bedtime.'

'And some days she would be there, and you would never arrive at all.'

'Yes, that happened. I suppose it must have happened quite often really.'

'Go back a little, then. How long have you known the Johnstones?'

'I've known of them ever since I qualified and went to work for Dr Trevelyan. Something like four years. But he's their doctor, I never had occasion to visit the house until about two years ago, when the little girl had mumps. That's when I met Kate.'

'She had never been to the surgery, either alone or with one of the children?'

'Johnstone wasn't a National Health patient, none of his family were. A doctor should know his place in the scheme of things. Even Trevelyan, who is by way of being a friend of the family.'

'I see. And on this first meeting . . . was it love at first sight?'

'I haven't said . . oh, well, if you must have it, I suppose there was an attraction.'

'Which grew into love?'

Again there was that wary glance at his solicitor. 'In the circumstances I should like to be able to deny that, but I can't.'

'Did you visit her at home?'

'In the course of my professional duties – '

'You're being evasive again, Dr Collingwood. Was Mrs Johnstone your patient?'

'Never. Not even in the sense that I attended her in place of Dr Trevelyan. As for being evasive,' – for the first time there was a touch of truculence in his tone – 'I don't know what else you expect.'

'Honesty,' said Maitland, and smiled suddenly. Not, thought Kells, watching him, at all an amused smile. He also thought that counsel's tone was sardonic as he added, 'or is that too much to ask?' A man who knew Maitland

29

better – Geoffrey Horton, for instance, – would have begun to sit up and take notice at that point. He might be blunt, and wasn't above trying to startle an admission out of a witness; but a client with whom he was completely out of sympathy would always be treated with the most exquisite courtesy.

'You said we'd leave my honesty out of it for the time being,' Collingwood reminded him stiffly. And then, as though it was too much of an effort to stay on his dignity, 'It's Kate, you see. How all this can be made to sound.'

'Mr O'Brien will have explained to her, as I have explained to you, that it is essential for the defence to know the worst that can be said.'

'Yes, I wonder – '

'You wonder whether she has been any more frank with him than you are being with me.'

'I – '

'Forget it. What's important is not your feelings at the moment, but the extent to which the prosecution will be able to prove some sort of liaison. So you must bear with me for the moment, Dr Collingwood. Did you ever attend Douglas Johnstone?'

'No. He wouldn't have stood for that.'

'Now, what is that meant to imply?'

Collingwood looked surprised. 'Only that Trevelyan was his doctor. He'd have thought it a come-down to be treated by a mere assistant.'

'Mr Kells will tell you that an answer like that, made thoughtlessly in court, could well be open to misconstruction.'

'But I've explained.'

'Counsel for the Prosecution might not give you the opportunity to explain. In fact, he almost certainly wouldn't.'

'Oh!' He thought about that for a moment. 'I suppose I must be very naïve about all this. I've thought a hundred times about how my story would sound in court, but I don't think I've ever faced the fact of being cross-examined.'

'Then think about it now. You must be very careful what you say, Dr Collingwood, careful even how you phrase your replies.'

'I suppose I must. That's bad enough. But will Kate have to give evidence?'

'That's up to O'Brien. But you'll find, after the prosecution witnesses are finished, that there will be questions that must be answered.'

'She's such an innocent, you see. I don't think she could cope with being cunning.'

'Then we must hope that the jury will take your view of her.'

'She's far more likely to tie herself into knots,' asserted Collingwood gloomily.

'There's nothing we can do about that at the moment. Let's get back to our matters of fact, things that are capable of proof. When you went professionally to the Johnstone home, then, it was to see the children?'

'That's right. The first time it happened by accident, because Dr Trevelyan was particularly busy; but I think, to tell you the truth, he's grown a little out of touch with his younger patients as he gets older. Anyway, I get on with Dougie and Janet all right, so it became an understood thing that I should look after them. Except for the occasional visit he'd make, as he did on the morning of Johnstone's death, to show he hadn't lost all interest in them.'

'Johnstone didn't object to this arrangement?'

'Not that I heard.'

'And how often did these visits of yours take place?'

'Very occasionally.'

'Over the period of two years you mentioned, can you give me an estimate of how many times you attended the children?'

'Without my records . . . say, five or six times. You could check that if it's important.'

'I think – ' said Maitland, glancing at Kells, who added

31

another note to his pad. 'Anything serious?' Antony went on, turning again to his client.

'I don't . . . oh, the children. The mumps was the worst thing, then they both had gastric 'flu once. After that, just the usual colds.'

'Wait a bit! That must have occasioned more than six visits.'

'I meant . . . you said, how often had I attended them, and I think there were about six different occasions. More visits than one for each illness, of course.'

'Yes, of course. More visits, perhaps, than might be considered strictly necessary.'

'That's a matter of judgement. In this case, mine.'

'Who did you see on these occasions, besides the patients?'

'Kate usually. She always worries frightfully. And the nursemaid invariably, I think.'

'Helen Gatsby,' said Kells. 'The prosecution are calling her,' he added morosely.

'I see. What can she tell them?' Maitland asked his client.

'She always seemed to like Kate.'

'That might not make any difference. She'll be on oath, and there are still some people who take that seriously, even apart from the possibility of being prosecuted for perjury.'

'Well, I think . . . she might have been conscious of something in the wind. Nothing – nothing overt.'

'Did you see Mrs Johnstone on these occasions, except in the presence of the nursemaid?'

'She would come downstairs with me, and give me coffee in the drawing-room if I wasn't in too much of a hurry. Or tea, if it was an afternoon call. Nothing wrong with that,' he added, with a sudden belligerence that made Maitland smile again.

'Nothing at all,' he agreed. 'But I should refrain from pointing that out to the court if I were you. That sort of thing is my job. But you'll be seeing Mr Kells again before the trial, he can put you right about all that kind of thing.'

'I'll try to remember,' said Collingwood, deflated.

'Good. Now, apart from these sick calls, did you ever visit Mrs Johnstone at her home?'

'Only that last day. I thought Dougie's cold was sufficient excuse, even though Dr Trevelyan had been in the morning.'

'Why did he do that, do you think? You said he was leaving the children to you.'

'There's only what I suggested just now . . . to show he hadn't lost all interest. Unless – '

'Well?'

'Do you think he might have heard some rumour, about Kate and me, I mean, and thought he'd better take over again?'

'Had he given you any cause to think that?'

'No. His manner was just as usual.'

'Then we'll hope your original guess was a good one. Why did *you* particularly want to visit Mrs Johnstone that afternoon?'

Collingwood hesitated. 'No particular reason. She hadn't been at the café for a day or two . . . of course I wanted to see her.'

'You saw Dougie too?'

'Yes.'

'Where is his bedroom in relation to the bathroom where Mr Johnstone left his syringe?'

'Good lord, I never thought of that. I could have done the whole thing myself, couldn't I?'

'Could you?'

'Well, actually no, because I haven't the faintest idea where any of the rooms are upstairs except the children's bedrooms and the nursery. Not on the same floor as their parents', I don't imagine. It's a tall house, and they're near the top. But it's a thought, all the same. Do you think you could suggest it to Mr O'Brien?'

Richard Kells started to protest at that, but Maitland

ignored him, giving his client a sour look. 'If you want to plead guilty, do so and have done with it,' he said. 'Tell Mr Kells, and he'll change my instructions. But I won't put up with any half-baked heroics.'

Collingwood considered that, not visibly abashed. 'Not a good idea,' he agreed at last.

'I'm glad you're showing at least so much sign of good sense,' Maitland told him. (Jenny would have complained that it was one of the occasions when he sounded very like Uncle Nick, but the mimicry, though accurate, was quite unconscious.) 'This last visit, now. You saw Dougie first. Did Mrs Johnstone accompany you?'

'No, but she came into the hall when I arrived, and told Sophie to bring tea to the drawing-room, she'd see me when I came down.'

'Sophie being – ?'

'The parlourmaid.'

'What time was this?'

'About three o'clock.'

'Were you long upstairs?'

'There was no need. Nurse told me Dr Trevelyan had been in the morning . . . well, I knew that anyway, but I didn't let on. So I went downstairs to Kate.'

'And you still say there was no special reason for your visit.'

'Only that . . . I told you I hadn't seen Kate for a day or two.'

'Could Sophie have overheard any of your conversation?'

'I suppose . . . when she brought the tea. Anyway, there was nothing to matter.'

'How long did you stay?'

'About twenty minutes.'

'What *did* you talk about?'

'I gathered she wasn't coming to the café that afternoon again. We argued about that a bit.'

'You say you hadn't seen her for a day of two. Did she give you any reason for that?'

'Only that Dougie wasn't well.'

'Did you think he was ill enough for that to constitute an excuse?'

'Well . . . no. That's why we argued, I suppose.'

'I see. What did Mrs Johnstone confide in you about her relationship with her husband?'

'Nothing much. I realised she wasn't happy, but she made no specific complaints.'

'You saw a great deal of her. You were in love with her – '

'I didn't say she was in love with me.'

There was a heavy kind of emphasis about that statement that seemed to invite the silence that followed. Maitland, engrossed in his witness, remembered Kells' presence suddenly and glanced in his direction. The solicitor, in his turn, was regarding his friend and client with a puzzled look. Antony admitted to some doubt himself, was that an admission that the man hated to make, or was it another lie? The only thing he could be sure of was that there was pain behind the words. 'If she didn't talk to you, whom might she have confided in?' he asked, with a return to his earlier abruptness.

'I don't know.'

'Some woman friend who was close to her, perhaps.' Collingwood only shook his head. Kells said tentatively, as if he doubted the reception his suggestion would receive:

'What about Jean Lamb?'

Collingwood gave him a rather weary look. 'I suppose that's possible,' he said unenthusiastically. Antony turned to the solicitor for enlightenment.

'I hadn't realised you knew the Johnstones yourself.'

'I didn't. But Mrs Lamb was having dinner with Kate Johnstone one evening at Ralstone's, when James and I were there together. Her husband was Douglas Johnstone's partner and they were at some gathering together in the city. I thought then she seemed a gentle, sympathetic person, a good listener, just the sort to receive confidences. And I should add,' he went on, but now he was avoiding Collingwood's eye, 'that the prosecution will be calling her.'

That brought Maitland, who had kept nobly to his chair all this time, on to his feet. The narrow room didn't allow much scope for movement. Two paces to the wall on his right, four paces to the one opposite. He came back to stand behind his chair, gripping the topmost of the wooden bars that formed its back until his knuckles showed white. 'I hope to heaven,' he said in an oddly quiet tone, 'that you're wrong about her, one way or another.'

That brought a protest from his client. 'But Jean is a friend of Kate's.'

'I already explained . . . have you ever been in a court of law, Dr Collingwood?'

'No.'

'Well, I can assure you, Mrs Lamb sounds just the sort of witness prosecuting counsel will revel in, even in direct examination. Who's got the case? Garfield, of course. Well then!'

'I have to agree with you,' said Kells slowly. 'But she may not have anything to tell, you know.'

'Perhaps not. Who do *you* think killed Douglas Johnstone?' he added, whirling back on his client again.

'Now, that's something I can answer. I haven't the faintest idea,' said Collingwood, sounding all at once much more confident.

'Nothing that Mrs Johnstone ever mentioned – ?'

'She talked of their friends, sometimes. I don't think any of them was particularly close to her except Jean. And she talked of her parents, but they were . . . they *approved* of Johnstone,' said Collingwood, with an emphasis that confirmed strongly the opinion his counsel had already formed as to his feelings for the dead man. 'Kate might be able to help you about this, of course,' the prisoner went on, 'but I don't see why any of them – '

36

'Never mind. There's just one more question, Dr Collingwood, and then we'll leave it for the present. About the morphine – '

Collingwood broke in before he could finish. 'I can't understand it,' he burst out, 'and what's more neither can Dr Trevelyan.'

'I thought when a check was made there was a certain amount of latitude.'

'Well, there is. You can stress that, I explained it to Richard. But the thing is, there shouldn't have been any missing when the stuff was never used.'

'Never?'

'That's what it amounts to.'

'But if an injection is given by the doctor, or in his presence and on his instructions, no record need be kept . . . or so I understand. Surely that can account for a discrepancy.'

'In anybody else's surgery, yes, I'd agree with you, though perhaps not to the amount that was missing. But Dr Trevelyan is positively rabid on the possibility of addiction, and he's quite positive, Richard tells me, that he never used any. The trouble is, neither did I. Being in his employ, I naturally followed his wishes on the subject. You can talk about spillage all you like, I don't think it will be convincing.'

'In that case, how do you explain – ?'

'I don't.'

'At least you can tell me where the stuff is kept.' Maitland's tone was unnaturally calm.

'There's a special wing built on to the side of the house, not very large, space is at a premium in that part of town. Waiting-room and my surgery downstairs, and a cubicle for the receptionist; examination room and Dr Trevelyan's surgery upstairs.'

'Any way through into the house?'

'A door on each floor.'

'You still haven't told me where the drugs are kept.'

'In a locked cupboard in Dr Trevelyan's room. Glass-fronted, easy enough to identify even by a stranger, but not easy of access.'

'A patient – ?'

'Most of his patients are fee-paying, like the Johnstones, and expect to be attended at home.'

'So that, perhaps, his surgery is left unoccupied a good part of the time?'

'Yes, that's certainly true. But I can't think how one of my patients could have found his way upstairs.'

'Did Mrs Johnstone ever – ?'

'No!'

The snapped reply appeared to restore Maitland's good humour. He smiled at his client, released his hold on the chair-back, and began to move towards the door. 'We won't try your patience any longer, Dr Collingwood,' he said, at his most formal. 'Mr Kells will arange it if I want to see you again.'

'At least you can be certain of finding me in.' Kells was already at the door, but Collingwood, although he too had risen, seemed uncertain of what was expected of him. If there was a question in his mind, however, he didn't ask it. Maitland came to a stop beside him and held out his hand.

'O'Brien has promised to arrange for me to see Mrs Johnstone tomorrow,' he said. Collingwood's eyes lightened suddenly, but still the question remained unuttered. But their handshake seemed to both men the sealing of a bargain.

Maitland was inclined to be silent on his way back to town. He only hoped he wouldn't regret later his part in the unspoken compact.

III

He was even later home than he expected, and apart from running the gauntlet of Gibbs's disapproval in the hall was allowed only one glass of sherry before Jenny called them to the table. As she had predicted, Sir Nicholas and Lady Harding had arrived before their host. He made his apologies, but neither of them seemed much disturbed at being kept waiting. Dinner proceeded smoothly, and it was not until they were settled with their coffee in front of the fire, and Antony was wondering whether Jenny had remembered to order more brandy, that his uncle referred obliquely to the reason for his lateness. Sir Nicholas was a man as tall as his nephew, though much more heavily built; with hair fair enough to conceal the fact that it was greying, and a naturally authoritative manner of which he was quite unconscious. At the moment, however, he seemed pleasantly relaxed, and though Antony and Jenny had no doubt at all where his questions might lead, they both thought that in all probability Vera was to some extent deceived by his manner. In which they underestimated their new aunt. Vera was a quick learner.

Sir Nicholas was beginning his careful preparations for the enjoyment of a cigar. Jenny had restored the dining-table to its customary neatness. Vera, who had learned by now not to jump up with an offer of help, was watching her husband, rather as though studying a skill that she might have need of some day. Maitland, having found to his relief that the supply of his uncle's favourite cognac had been replenished, had carried his find to the writing table in the corner where the glasses were already set out.

'You won't need telling, Antony, that Mallory isn't pleased with you,' remarked Sir Nicholas, making his selection at last.

'He made that quite clear,' responded his nephew drily.

'It might be interesting to know' – the older man's tone was reflective – 'what form his displeasure took . . . on this occasion.' He was perfectly well aware of the clerk's attitude, just as Maitland had long since despaired of getting what another man might have felt was a proper respect from old Mr Mallory.

'He accepted that Breach of Contract thing for me, and then had the cheek to say he was sure that was in accordance with my wishes,' Antony said, but the amusement underlying the rueful tone was not lost upon his uncle. 'It's as dull as ditchwater, of course, and nothing in my line nowadays, so I'll have to do some work on it.'

'Your achievements in that field were not inconsiderable at one time,' Sir Nicholas reminded him. Which drew a startled look; perhaps it was as well that Maitland had finished pouring. Vera, however, who realised as well as he did that any compliment implied in the remark was incidental, but also realised that it was part of her husband's policy of educating her in all matters concerning her new family, accepted a glass with a murmur of thanks and added in her rather elliptical way.

'Might be interesting to hear about.'

Antony had had the greatest respect for her abilities when she was practising at the bar, but this was too much for him. 'Dull,' he said again. Vera was a tall, solidly built woman, with thick, dark hair streaked with grey and already, thus early in the evening, beginning to escape from its confining pins. That was all as it had been as long as he had known her, but there were certain changes besides. Her dress was still sack-like, but a sack with some pretensions to elegance now, and of a becoming shade of blue. Maitland eyed her with affection, even as the finality of his tone implied a denial of her request. Now that he had resolved his doubts as to the propriety of continuing to share his uncle's household, even on the partially detached basis that had been devised so many years ago, now that Sir Nicholas was actually married, he was able to take a simple pleasure in Vera's presence and to find a very real amusement in her slightly original ways of dealing with her husband's unpredictable moods. But not even Vera could suppress Sir Nicholas altogether.

So now, ignoring the exchange between his wife and his

40

nephew, he reached for the box of Swan Vestas and his tone became silky. 'I agree, of course, that lately your energies have been largely engaged in other, and perhaps less desirable, ways. Which brings us back to this present venture. Another murder,' he mused. Which was decidedly unfair, considering that his own was largely a criminal practice.

'A sordid, domestic affair,' said Jenny, coming to seat herself beside Vera on the sofa. The phrase seemed to have taken her fancy. The tray was already in place; as Antony finished passing the glasses he came to her side to distribute the coffee. She gave him a warm, conspiratorial smile as she passed him Vera's cup. 'No harm in it at all, Uncle Nick,' she said reassuringly.

'I am glad to have your warranty on that point, of course.' There were gaps between the words as he applied the match and drew on his cigar. 'At the same time I should like to point out that there are certain particulars about the matter that require – shall we say? – clarification.'

'It was all quite clear,' said Jenny, 'until you started obscuring it. There are two defendants. Kevin O'Brien is acting for one of them, and he persuaded Antony to take on the other. Without a fee, I know, but – '

'That point is irrelevant,' said Sir Nicholas, as she had known he would. The cigar was drawing satisfactorily now, an even glow. 'It wasn't really O'Brien's place to act as intermediary.'

'Except that he believes his client is innocent,' said Antony. 'Which inclines him to believe – though, admittedly, it isn't proof positive – that my client is innocent too.'

'That is precisely the point I am trying to make to you. What do you think about it, my dear?' he asked, turning suddenly to Vera . . . a man crushed under the weight of a younger generation's misunderstanding. 'It is a blatant request for Antony to engage in one of his fact-finding missions, that's what I object to. Besides, I cannot think that O'Brien

41

will be altogether a good influence on a man of Antony's temperament.'

'What's wrong with him?'

'One member of the partnership should show some signs of level-headedness,' said Sir Nicholas crushingly.

'I made it quite clear to him,' said Maitland, unmoved by these strictures, 'that I wouldn't undertake anything beyond the simple study of my brief unless I thought there were good grounds for further investigation.'

'And having seen your client, as I gather you did this evening?'

'There are some questions that need answering.'

'You've convinced yourself, probably before you even saw him, that he's telling you the truth.'

'On the contrary, I'm convinced he told me at least three lies. All the same – '

'Don't see your point, I'm afraid,' Vera put in. After years of participating in such discussions, she had not Jenny's knack of sitting quietly while controversy raged around her. Perhaps also she was afraid of an explosion from her husband if she left any comment to him.

Antony smiled at her. 'Do you remember Fran Gifford?' he asked. It was over Miss Gifford's defence that they had first met, when Vera was still at the bar herself.

'Of course I do.'

'She told us some lies in the beginning, but as it turned out . . . what I'm trying to say is, he may be lying about some things, and still not be guilty of murder.'

Vera gave him her rather grim smile, which in the early days of their acquaintance had had a quite devastating effect on his morale. 'Shouldn't have let you go on if *I*'d believed she was lying,' she told him.

'All the same – ' said Maitland again.

This time it was his uncle who interrupted him. 'Nobody can deny the truth of your assertion,' he agreed. 'But you know perfectly well I don't approve of these *extra-curricular*

42

activities of yours. However well intentioned,' he added, and leaned back in his chair as though the matter were closed.

As indeed it might have been. It was Jenny who unwittingly stirred things up again, saying indignantly, 'That's not fair, Uncle Nick. *You* haven't been above using Antony in the background when it suited you.'

'Generally, however, at his own instigation. You will agree with me, my dear,' he said, turning so sharply to Vera that he almost lost the ash from his cigar, 'those cases on your circuit – '

'As much my fault as Antony's,' Vera conceded. 'Not yours.'

This was not at all what Sir Nicholas had intended to elicit, and Jenny was tempted to laugh at his expression. Instead, being in no mood to brush things under the rug, she went on firmly. 'You wouldn't remember, Vera. Barbara!' And this was an undoubted hit, because Barbara Wentworth, now Barbara Stringer, had certainly been Sir Nicholas's client before Maitland ever heard of her.

Sir Nicholas laid down his cigar carefully, and picked up his coffee cup, which Jenny had remembered tonight to fill to the precise level he insisted on, one quarter inch below the rim. 'You seem to be trying to prove something,' he said mildly, 'I'm not quite sure what it is.'

It was clear from Jenny's expression that she had almost lost sight of this herself. 'Only that it's quite reasonable for Mr O'Brien to want Antony's help,' she said, after a slight hesitation. 'And that it's an ordinary case, not a dangerous one, I mean.' But Antony realised, with a slight sinking of the spirits, that it was herself she was trying to convince, not them.

'If you are relying on the Wentworth case as a precedent – ' said Sir Nicholas.

'It's a good one,' said Jenny, bristling.

'I am constrained to remind you that in the course of it some man whose name I cannot now recall tried to murder

43

your husband. In chambers,' he added, as though that was the final straw.

'But there was no need to worry,' said Antony cheerfully. He wasn't quite sure what had got into Jenny, but dimly felt she needed some reassurance. 'Uncle Nick hit him over the head with a copy of the Law Reports, or some such thing – '

'Which Mallory handed me,' said Sir Nicholas; he had relaxed again now, and seemed to be enjoying the recollection.

'Yes, that's another thing he'll never forgive me, which on the whole is unfair,' Antony agreed.

Vera was looking at her husband. There was a gleam of amusement in her eye. 'Told me about the case, never told me *that*,' she averred.

'It was an incident I prefer to forget.' (But Antony was suddenly convinced that there might be some laughter about it later when these two were alone.) 'However, Jenny – Sir Nicholas was not likely to lose touch with the point of a conversation – 'I think you mistake the cause of my anxiety. It is not Antony's safety, that is not likely to be at risk in a domestic problem, as you pointed out. But it is not going to do his reputation any good to lose a case with which he is known to have identified himself so thoroughly. And now he tells us his client has been lying to him.'

'Back to square one,' said Jenny flippantly, but it was evident that his discourse had cheered her. She glanced round to see that none of the coffee cups was empty, and then curled herself up more comfortably in her corner of the sofa. 'Go on, Antony, tell us what these lies were. If you won't have pity on my curiosity, think of Vera and Uncle Nick.'

'And how do they affect the defence?' said Sir Nicholas, retrieving his cigar.

'I'll have to outline the prosecution case for you before I explain that.' He did so, briefly, and for once in his life

44

Sir Nicholas listened without comment. 'I asked for explanations, of course,' said Maitland in conclusion, 'and it was there that I think my client departed from the truth.'

'In what way?'

'Well, first he told us Kate Johnstone had made no special complaints to him about her marriage. *I* think she chattered to him about it like a magpie.'

'Intuition?' enquired Sir Nicholas coldly.

'Guesswork,' Antony admitted, knowing well enough that anything of that nature was anathema to his uncle. 'He did say he knew the marriage wasn't a happy one, but he must have known any one of a dozen people could tell me as much. He also lied – all right, Uncle Nick, I'm not sure of these things, I can't be – I think he also lied when he said there was no particular reason for his going to Wilgrave Square on the afternoon of the murder, other than the fact that he hadn't seen Mrs Johnstone for several days. I have a feeling that perhaps some sort of a climax had been reached in their relationship, so that, from his own point of view at least, he had a pretty good reason for wanting to see her.'

He paused there, looking round his audience. Sir Nicholas deposited an inch and a half of ash from his cigar. 'And the third lie?' he asked idly.

'He denied that Mrs Johnstone had committed adultery with him. I admit, it wouldn't have been easy for them, but in this matter I'm afraid of what the police may turn up.' Watching Sir Nicholas's expression he added hurriedly, 'I don't blame him for that, Uncle Nick. He's only trying to shield her.'

'And this is the couple on whom you and O'Brien propose to squander your valuable time,' said Sir Nicholas bitterly. 'Is there any indication at all that this is other than what it seems . . . a domestic killing; sordid, as Jenny so aptly put it?'

'You realise it's likely that Garfield, as Solicitor General, will lead for the prosecution,' said Antony casually. His uncle gave him a sharp look, and Vera a puzzled one, because it was so very obvious that in some way this was meant as an answer to his uncle's objection.

'Should like to understand that, Antony,' Vera said after a moment.

'Well, you see, Garfield has a particularly strict sense of morality. You'll bear me out in that, Uncle Nick?'

'I will, but – '

'He needs someone to counteract that, to point out to the court that it's murder they're trying, not morals.'

'And you and O'Brien between you should find yourselves eminently fitted for the task,' said Sir Nicholas nastily.

'Come to that, I really don't see Dr James Collingwood as being particularly depraved,' Maitland assured him. Whether his uncle listened to this or not, he underwent one of his bewildering changes of mood.

'If we consider O'Brien's character and your own, Antony, it should be instructive to watch you tackling a joint defence,' he said genially. And it was only much later, when he and Vera were leaving, that he added what must have been a rider to that remark. 'The object, after all, is not to provide amusement for your colleagues at the Bar,' he said, as though no other subject of conversation had arisen in the interim. 'But I still consider that questioning is not the mode of conversation among gentlemen.'

WEDNESDAY, 17th NOVEMBER

I

Jenny reverted to that the next morning. She let Antony have his breakfast in peace, but he was conscious all the time of something unsaid, and finally, when she had poured his third cup of coffee, he asked her, 'What's up, love?' But he sounded negligent, and perhaps it was this that prompted her to a tone she did not ordinarily employ. 'Johnson!' she said tragically.

'Johnstone?' He sounded genuinely puzzled, but Jenny was in no mood to make allowances.

'No, of course not. Uncle Nick, last night. He was quoting Dr Johnson,' she explained.

'Oh, that! I expect it was just the similarity in names that put him in mind of his favourite quotation.'

'I don't think so at all. You know it always means trouble.'

'But in this case . . . no, really, Jenny love, you said yourself – '

'You know perfectly well Uncle Nick gets feelings about things.'

'Well, yes, but . . . he explained that. He wouldn't mind my accepting the brief and losing the verdict in the ordinary way. After all, it happens all the time. It's only if I'm known to have identified myself too thoroughly with my client's interests that he thinks an adverse verdict might be damaging.'

'I see.' That was one of Antony's phrases she had borrowed, and she used it doubtfully. But then she brightened. 'I expect I shouldn't have stressed the squalid nature of the affair. But it's such a comfort – '

Maitland was following his own train of thought. 'Uncle Nick is a strange mixture,' he said. 'For someone so tolerant – '

'Tolerant?' repeated Jenny with something dangerously like a giggle. 'In some ways he's almost as bad as Mr Garfield.'

'Come now, that's very unfair. Think about it, love. He chooses to take a high moral tone with us; when I was in my teens he took his responsibilities as a substitute parent very seriously, let me tell you. Also it did cross my mind last night that he might be afraid of shocking Vera, which is nonsense, of course, she's been at the Bar nearly as long as he has. All the same, he's had far too much experience of human nature not to make allowances for its vagaries.'

'I suppose you're right. Antony, what do you think happened if those two are innocent?'

'Heaven and Earth!' He drank the rest of his coffee, and got to his feet. 'I'd better be getting on, Jenny. We're due at Holloway at eleven, and there are things to be done before that.'

'You didn't answer my question.'

'How can I know? To begin with, I don't know the first thing about Douglas Johnstone yet, let alone anything about his habits.'

Jenny picked up the coffee pot and shook it, and then piled her cup and saucer resignedly on top of her plate. 'Oh, well!' she said. 'Who lives may learn,' and gave him a grin to show she knew she was quoting his own words at him again.

II

O'Brien, with his customary energy, had arranged transportation and picked Antony up from chambers a little before he was ready to embark on the expedition. In the car he introduced Maitland to David Shaw, his instructing solicitor. An elderly man who might have been made up for the part of family lawyer and who certainly disapproved of the whole matter in general, and perhaps of Antony's part in it in particular. 'But there is no question, you know, of a joint defence,' he said fussily, as the limousine pulled away from the kerb. 'In the circumstances – '

'Let's leave the circumstances to look after themselves for the moment.' Kevin O'Brien's spirits were quite clearly high this morning, and Maitland took time to envy him his light-heartedness in the face of the interview that lay before them. 'Maitland is here in an advisory capacity. Nothing wrong with that.' His tone was specious, and the solicitor sniffed his disapproval.

'So long as you realise the position,' he said in a martyred tone. 'There can be no question of my sanctioning anything contrary to my clients' instructions.'

O'Brien caught Maitland's eye. Antony could not have sworn to it but he was pretty sure that his colleague winked at him. This did nothing to raise his own spirits, but he was aware that there should have been some amusement in the reflection that Mr Shaw was not likely to be representing Kate Johnstone very much longer. However, that was O'Brien's problem. He turned his eyes deliberately on the familiar scene beyond the car window, and tried not to conjure up in advance the unmistakable smell of a women's prison, which is unlike anything else in the world, or to anticipate the feeling of claustrophobia that was going to oppress him as one door after another was locked behind them. It was a long time now since it had been agony for him to sit with the door closed, but he doubted now that he would ever be entirely free of the memories that he tried so hard to suppress.

And, unlike yesterday's experience, Mrs Johnstone was produced with commendable speed. She was a small, slightly built woman with a cloud of dark hair and grey eyes that immediately made him think of Jenny, though he could not have said at that point where the resemblance lay. She came in quietly, greeted David Shaw with a sort of gentle deference in her manner that seemed to suggest that he was a long time family friend; spoke more formally to Kevin O'Brien, and then turned her eyes on the stranger, not waiting for an introduction. 'You must be Mr Maitland,' she said. 'I'm so glad you're going to help James.'

He thought of warning her then, as he had warned his own client, that she might not like his questions, but that could be dealt with when it arose. There was a strength about her . . . even at that early stage in their acquaintance he wondered about the propriety of James Collingwood's description of her. But, of course, to a man in love . . .

'I think,' said Mr Shaw – and, of course, it was quite correct that he should take charge of the proceedings – 'that this very irregular interview will proceed more smoothly if we all sit down.' Kate obeyed him immediately, Maitland let O'Brien have the place at the head of the table, and himself sat at the side, opposite the solicitor; but his attention was already all for the prisoner.

'You know why I wanted this talk,' O'Brien was saying.

'For Mr Maitland's information.' It was a hopeful sign, Antony thought, that she answered readily and did not seem to resent his presence.

'Yes, of course. What I wanted to explain to you is that you may be called upon to repeat yourself . . . to answer again things that I have already asked you, I mean. But from his point of view – '

'I have a weakness for getting my facts at first hand,' Antony told her when Kevin did not seem to be going to complete his sentence. 'And Mr Shaw has been kind enough to agree.' If there was to be plain speaking as a result of this interview, as he felt in his bones there would be, that was none of his affair. In the meantime, the proprieties might as well be observed.

Kate Johnstone directed a look at her solicitor that, fleetingly, was neither gentle, nor deferential. But when she turned back to Maitland again it was with very little sign of emotion of any kind. 'I didn't kill my husband', she stated flatly.

Antony acknowledged that merely with an inclination of his head. At that moment he wouldn't have given you odds either way, but of one thing he was already certain. If the Harleys thought their daughter had been a reluctant partner in any plot to kill her husband, they were wrong. Of the two accused, she was by far the stronger character. 'Then who do you think did?' he asked idly. Mr Shaw thought perhaps the question was indicative of lack of interest and began to hope that, after all, his friends the Harleys might be going to get their own way. But O'Brien, who knew Maitland better (though not quite as well as he thought he did), sat back and prepared to efface himself. That casual manner concealed, he knew, a clear enough mind.

The reply had come quickly. 'Not James,' said Kate, equally positively.

Again there was no direct comment on the statement. 'Tell me about your married life,' Maitland suggested.

'I wasn't happy with Douglas. The servants will tell you there were quarrels.'

And that is the only reason you are admitting it to me. But, in spite of that realisation, there was a directness about her that he liked. 'Go back to the beginning,' he said. 'When did you marry him? And why?'

There was a quick frown for that. 'That's a funny question,' she said.

'All the same, I should like to know the answer.'

'We were married ten years ago. As for why, I could say, "the usual reason".'

He smiled at her. 'Would that be true?'

'I think . . . in a way. I was eighteen and . . . you want the

51

truth, don't you? The whole truth and nothing but the truth?'

'Nicely put.'

O'Brien, watching them, thought for a moment she was going to challenge the amusement in Maitland's tone. Instead she told him seriously, 'I wasn't happy at home, desperate to get away, if you must know. And Douglas . . . he was fifteen years older, good looking, a man of the world. That's what I thought then. I suppose he dazzled me.'

'And your parents approved of the marriage?'

'That should have warned me, shouldn't it?' She was showing a trace of humour now herself but it was gone when she continued her narrative. 'The glamour didn't last long. I found him a dour man; that would have been his own word, but of course he would never have thought of applying it to himself. He hadn't any formal religion, but a mass of preju- dices, even more than I had left my parents' house to escape. I remember – ' she hesitated. 'You can't be interested in all this.'

'Believe me, I am.'

She still didn't reply immediately, Her eyes were fixed on his face, as though assessing the truth of his words. When at last she spoke her voice was lower. 'He had never seen me wearing makeup of course, or perfume, but I thought now it would be all right. I started with some rather expensive scent. He broke the bottle and the bedroom reeked for days. And, of course, that went on reminding him – '

'Was he a violent man?'

'If you mean, did he knock me about? No, he didn't.' Surprisingly her lips quivered on the edge of a smile. 'I think it was touch and go once or twice, though. I must have been a dreadful trial to him. But – don't you see? – he wanted a completely docile wife to entertain, to run his household, to bear his children. I was quite prepared to keep my part of the bargain, though it meant the constant suppression of all my natural instincts. But nothing I could do was ever good

52

enough, which I suppose isn't surprising. I'm a very ordinary woman, Mr Maitland, not a saint.'

Part of that statement at least was true. He was not so sure about the ordinary. 'Didn't it make any difference when the children came?'

'No, because . . . they were just another cause of dissension. Dougie isn't strong; Dr Trevelyan says he'll grow out of it and James agrees with him, but Douglas insisted on quite a severe regime – to make a man of him, he said – and he thought I coddled him.' Her voice had softened as she spoke of the child and for the first time Maitland saw her as vulnerable. 'Well,' – she shrugged, and again there was that flickering smile – 'perhaps he wasn't so far wrong.'

'And the little girl?' Maitland was absorbed in his witness and the fact that she seemed to be talking freely now, and hadn't even a thought to spare for O'Brien's unnatural silence.

'Janet? Oh that was quite a different matter. A tomboy and he wanted a Dresden doll. You see – you really do see, don't you, Mr Maitland? – there was absolutely no pleasing him.'

Two unhappy people; and why, if she was innocent, was she painting her husband in the blackest hues she could find? James Collingwood had had more sense, or had she really been as discreet in that relationship as the doctor had implied? Almost as if she had read his thought she said into the small silence, 'I shouldn't be denigrating Douglas. He was a good man according to his own lights. It might be fairer to say I couldn't live up to him.'

'Did the thought of a separation, of divorce perhaps, ever cross your mind?'

'Not until – ' She broke off there, looking from one of her lawyers to the other; at David Shaw, stiff and disapproving; at Kevin O'Brien, who gave her a warm, inspiriting smile.

'Sure now, and you may as well tell us,' said Kevin encouragingly. Maitland was too intent even to notice an affectation that would normally have irritated him; though he

53

remembered it well enough later, even to the extent of adding the words 'me darling' to the sentence when he recounted the conversation to Jenny.

Perhaps it was this injunction, perhaps she just had a natural sense of honesty. Kate hesitated a moment and then said firmly, 'Until I met James.'

'I see. That was two years ago, he tells me. How long was it before you began to realise – '

'That I was in love with him?' She seemed almost eager now to give herself away. 'Not for some time, of course. I think it was about six months ago that I first mentioned the question of divorce to Douglas.'

'And what was his reaction to that?'

'He was furious. He had no idea, you see. Of course I didn't tell him that . . . well, that there was somebody else.'

'So nothing was decided?'

'No. I thought I'd let him get used to the idea and then try again.'

'And – ?'

'I talked to him in September, near the beginning of the month as far as I remember. This time he was ready for me, very cold and formal. He said he preferred to avoid a scandal, and had no intention of making an arranged divorce possible for me. There was something – oh, he was so *icy* – I lost my temper at that point. I don't often, it always leaves me slightly ashamed and sick, but I told him straight I would leave him myself and take the children with me. And he . . . he laughed at me, Mr Maitland. He said in that case he would divorce me; he could prove adultery and there was no question but that he would be given custody of Dougie and Janet.'

'Who was he going to name as co-respondent?'

'James.'

'That's awkward, isn't it? And could he . . . prove adultery, I mean?'

He thought she paled at that, but the light in the room was harsh and took away in any case what little colour she

54

had. 'I suppose he had been having me followed, and he admitted he'd been paying one of the servants . . . Sophie, I suppose. But there were only the meetings at the teashop, and when James came to the house, of course. Nothing could have been made out of that.'

'Did Dr Collingwood know you were contemplating divorce?'

'Yes I . . . we were always honest with each other.'

'What was his reaction to that last conversation you have described?'

'We were . . . unhappy, Mr Maitland. But James recognised as well as I did that Douglas was in the right of it, in spite of – ' She stopped there, abruptly, but this time her eyes remained fixed on Maitland with a horrified expression which was unmistakable. Perhaps she had forgotten they were not alone in the room.

'Come now, Mrs Johnstone, a little of that honesty you were talking about.' Maitland had his own forms of encouragement for an unwilling witness, and they were not O'Brien's. In this instance, however, they seemed to work almost as well.

Kate said, so softly that even in the quiet room he had to strain his ears to hear her, 'Douglas said again he didn't want a scandal, I could stay if I liked. But I wasn't to think it would matter terribly if I went, he had often thought he'd like a free hand with Dougie and Janet. So, of course, I stayed. He wouldn't be consciously cruel, Mr Maitland, but children at that age – at any age – need some affection. Besides, I couldn't get on without them.'

'But you say there have been no incidents that your husband could cite?'

'Even without that, a case in court could have done James irreparable harm.'

'So things went on as before?'

'Yes.'

55

'Mr Johnstone made no objections to Dr Collingwood treating the children when it was necessary?'

'He might not have known.'

'The maid – ?'

'Oh, yes, Sophie. I suppose she told him, but he never mentioned the fact.'

'Tell me about the children.' He was abrupt again, perhaps because he knew the question touched a sensitive spot.

'There isn't much to tell. Dougie is eight now, I told you he is delicate, but I can watch him growing stronger every year. Janet, who is six, is good for him. She's lively and happy, at least I'm glad they're able to be together.'

'Are they with your parents?'

'No.' Even though she was obviously moved by this line of questioning a faint smile appeared again on her lips. 'I suppose it's terrible to say I'm glad about that but as I'm the one that seems to be in the wrong they could hardly insist on getting the guardianship. Charles – that's Douglas's brother – and his wife Felicity have taken them in for the time being. They promised me they'll look after them if I can't go home. But that isn't really much comfort, Mr Maitland, they need me as much as I need them.'

There was a pause after that. Antony took a moment to look at his companions; at Kevin O'Brien, so unusually silent; and at the solicitor, who still had his disapproving look. 'That brings us to the day of the murder,' he said at last, turning again to the woman on his right.

'What do you want to know?'

'Well, as to opportunity, we'll talk about yours first.'

'I suppose that's reasonable,' she said sadly.

'I'm afraid it is. Dr Collingwood came to see you, we'll come to that in a minute. So there is no doubt he *could* have handed over the morphine, and later you were seen coming out of your husband's room.'

'That was Sophie again, the one Douglas had asked to spy on me.'

'She said she was surprised.'

'That was because we'd had separate rooms for months.'

'And your reason for being there? Mr O'Brien told me, but I'd like to hear it from you as well.'

'It's awful to have to admit that the servants took sides in our differences, Mr Maitland. But they did, and my maid Daisy was the only one besides Nurse who was on my side. I don't really need very much looking after, and Daisy was supposed to see to Douglas's things too, small repairs, sewing on buttons, things like that. But I was afraid she'd been growing slack about it, so I thought I'd better check up, and it happened that I chose that afternoon.'

'The bathroom where he left the syringe was off his bedroom, was it?'

'Yes.' She paused and then added a little desperately, 'I could have gone in, but I didn't.'

'Then tell me about Dr Collingwood's visit.'

'He came to see Dougie.'

'On the contrary, Mrs Johnstone, he came to see you.'

'Mr Maitland – ' she protested and suddenly it was his turn to smile at her.

'He admitted as much to me, Mrs Johnstone, and I think I can take his word for it. Was there any particular reason that he wanted to see you?'

'Not really.'

'Come now, you can do better than that. He told me you hadn't been to the assignation in the teashop for several days.'

'I hate that word,' said Kate a little petulantly. 'I hadn't been and I didn't intend to go again. I told him that the last time I saw him.'

'I see. And having made this decision, how did you feel about it?'

She closed her eyes for a moment as though the memory was too painful. 'Dreadful,' she said. 'Dreadful! But it was the only thing to be done. I was afraid for James, I told you about that. And I was terrified of losing the children.'

'Did Dr Collingwood know where your husband's bathroom was?'

'No, how could he? He was never upstairs except on the nursery floor.' She was speaking rather quickly now, and her tone had sharpened. 'You *are* on his side, aren't you?' she asked, almost belligerently. 'I'd never have talked to you if I hadn't believed that.'

'I am on his side, and that seems to mean I'm on yours too,' he assured her. 'But Mr Shaw and Mr O'Brien will already have explained to you that we have to know the worst.'

'But – '

'Tell me about the servants,' he said quickly.

'They were Douglas's not mine,' she said. 'All except Daisy, who came to me when I was married; and Nurse, of course, who was engaged after Dougie was born.'

'Were any of them remembered in your husband's will?'

'I don't know, but it seems very unlikely. He paid well, but he wasn't an over-generous man.'

'I made it my business to enquire into that,' said David Shaw, speaking for the first time. 'There were no such legacies.' He still sounded as disapproving as ever, but Maitland was glad he was willing to co-operate to even so small an extent.

'And none of them had any grudge against your husband?' he insisted.

'Nobody that I can think of.'

'And nobody had recently been dismissed,' Shaw put in. 'In any event, how could they have obtained the morphine?'

'That's a difficult question anyway, unless we admit Dr Collingwood supplied it. And I'm not prepared to do that.' There was a definiteness in Maitland's voice that hadn't been there before and both the other two men glanced at him

58

sharply. 'Did you have any visitors that day?' he asked, turning to Kate again.

'Charles came to lunch.'

'Charles Johnstone, your brother-in-law?'

'That's right.'

'Was that by pre-arrangement?'

'Yes. Douglas meant to come home but he was held up by something or other at the office.'

'Your sister-in-law wasn't included in the invitation?'

'Of course she was, but she was going to a luncheon, some charity affair or other. So Charles and I lunched alone, and the children were allowed down to join us.'

In the last few minutes Maitland had found a tattered envelope in his pocket and was making notes on it. It looked as though they were illegible. Now he raised his head again. 'Would Mrs Felicity Johnstone have objected to their presence?' he asked.

'On the contrary. It was because Douglas wasn't there – he had certain times he liked to see the children, but not at lunch.'

'Were they close, those two . . . your husband and your brother-in-law?'

'Oh dear!' For the first time she detached her attention from Maitland and looked from one to the other of her lawyers. 'If I have to be honest – '

'As I said before, I should prefer it.'

'Well then, they were so different. Charles is an intensely human man, fond of children, fond of the good things in life. But Douglas had a sense of duty about such things as keeping in touch with his relations, and Charles was far too good-humoured ever to refuse an invitation.'

'I take it – this is something you can probably answer for me, Mr Shaw – that Charles Johnstone did not benefit financially from his brother's death.'

Again David Shaw inserted himself unwillingly into the conversation. 'He did not,' he said briefly.

59

O'Brien said nothing at all, but his eyes had turned from watching his client to concentrate on the play of expression on Maitland's face. Antony said, 'Thank you,' with equal brevity to the solicitor, and then spoke directly to Kate again. 'What is Charles Johnstone's profession?' he asked.

'He's one of the joint managing directors of Bramley's Bank.'

'Is he, though?' That would have done away with the financial motive even if one had existed. At least, he thought it would. 'Were the children with you all the time he was at Wilgrave Square?'

'No, we had a sherry together first and they came down and joined us at the table; and afterwards they left as soon as the meal was finished.'

'And – '

'Charles had coffee with me but he had to go to a meeting.'

'Were you together constantly then, while he was in the house?'

Afterwards he was not sure whether he had expected the question to distress her, but her answer came reluctantly. 'I don't like this at all, Mr Maitland.'

'Hadn't it occurred to you that if you and Dr Collingwood are innocent, as you have jointly and severally declared to us, someone else must be guilty?'

'But not . . . not someone I know so well, someone I'm fond of.'

'Think about it now,' he advised her.

'I don't need to think.'

'Then tell me what I want to know.' He was intent again on question and answer, but he was aware of Kevin O'Brien moving uneasily at the head of the table. Perhaps some of Kate's own emotion had communicated itself to her counsel. 'Come now,' Maitland added more persuasively. 'When we get into court we can ask your servants the same question.'

'Very well.' She didn't like it, but she gave in with comparative grace. 'He went upstairs just before he left, and it was his custom to use Douglas's bathroom.'

'And how long was he absent on this occasion?'

'Not long enough to be noticeable.'

'But he was familiar with your husband's medical condition, and habits?'

'I can't deny it.' But then she was protesting again. 'But all this is so silly, if you only knew – '

'What, Mrs Johnstone?'

'How ridiculous it is. Charles is the gentlest soul, he couldn't possibly hurt anyone.'

'I'll bear it in mind.'

'Well, I think you should.'

'And is Felicity also the gentlest soul? You'll forgive the familiarity, but with all these Johnstones about it seems less confusing.'

'Sentimental,' said Kate in a considering tone. 'Anyway, she wasn't there.'

'So I understand. Now it seems to me that somebody told me – was it you, O'Brien? – that there was a further visitor that day, Mrs Ernest Lamb.'

'Jean? Oh, yes, she was there, but you can't think – '

'You haven't given me anything yet to form a basis for thought, Mrs Johnstone. I'm more interested, to tell you the truth, in what you may have told her about your relationship with Dr Collingwood.'

Again his words seemed to dismay the prisoner. 'Why?' she demanded.

'Because if you were in any degree frank with her – '

'She wouldn't tell the police!'

'In court, she might not have the choice.'

'But she's . . . she's nice. She and Charles would make a good pair really, not an unkind thought about anybody.'

'That, unfortunately, is not the point. Was she in your confidence about your relationship with your husband?'

61

'She knew . . . oh, she knew that there was friction between us.'

'And that you had asked for a divorce?' Something in his tone may have alerted her to the fact that he was willing to wait all day for an answer. She looked around again, a little wildly this time, and then said with a dignity that Maitland found somehow pathetic, 'Yes, of course, I told her that too; we were always good friends.'

'Had you mentioned Dr Collingwood to her?'

'Only that he was attending the children. Not until that day.'

'You were upset after your talk with him. What did you tell her?'

'That I loved him. That I was not going to see him again.'

'How long did her visit last?'

'About an hour. She left not long before Douglas got home.'

'Without going upstairs?'

'She went upstairs, and I went with her.'

'So she had no opportunity of meddling with the syringe?'

'No, absolutely not. We went to my room, her hat and gloves were there.'

'And when your husband came home?'

'That was about ten to six. He seemed in a good mood, I was in the hall when he came in and he kissed me. He hadn't done that for a long time.'

'And then?'

'He went upstairs. It was time for his injection, or nearly. I didn't worry when he didn't come down again . . . well, I thought he had done and had gone to his study. It was the housemaid who found him, just before dinner time. She went into the room to turn down the bed. After that there was the doctor, and then much later the police. Does it do any good to think about all that, Mr Maitland?'

'Perhaps not.' He put away the stub of pencil he had been using and tucked the envelope back into his pocket. 'You

62

have been very patient with me, Mrs Johnstone, but I won't worry you any more just now.' He came to his feet as he spoke and Kate did too, turning a little, so that she could still face him as he went towards the door. He stopped squarely in front of her. 'I've already assured Dr Collingwood that I'll do my best for both of you,' he said. That was not strictly true, but he thought that when he left his client the assurance had been implicit in his manner.

Kate's eyes lighted at that and she stretched out a hand impulsively. 'Thank you!' she said. 'Oh, thank you! You see, if I was never to see any of them again . . . James, or Dougie, or Janet . . . I don't see how I could bear it.'

That that, at least, was true he never – either then or later – entertained the slightest doubt.

III

Mr Shaw's manner was more acid than ever after they left the prison, but Kevin O'Brien was in a boisterous mood and there was no declining his invitation to lunch. 'For I've got a table booked, ready and waiting at Astroff's,' he said, 'and there are things we must discuss.'

That might have been true, but there was an uncomfortable silence in the car as they drove back to town; and when they reached the restaurant Shaw declined any other refreshment than grapefruit juice, presumably in case alcohol might have a mellowing effect on his mood. 'Well now,' said Kevin O'Brien, when the waiter had brought their order and departed, 'it seems after all, Maitland, you're on my side of the fence.'

Antony made no immediate reply. David Shaw had obviously much that he wished to communicate and it was only too possible that he would suffer an apoplexy if the opportunity were denied him. Sure enough, he burst immediately into indignant speech.

'This is intolerable,' he said. 'I allowed this visit at your insistence, Mr O'Brien, but it was on the distinct understanding that nothing would be done that opposed my clients' wishes.'

'Now that's where you're wrong.' Whatever might be said about O'Brien's tone, it wasn't conciliatory. 'You may consider yourself pledged to the Harleys, Mr Shaw, but Kate Johnstone's my client and it's her wishes I have to consider. This business of pleading guilty – '

'Is the safest way for her, whatever it may be for *your* client, Mr Maitland.' There was no doubt about the intensity of Shaw's feelings and Kevin O'Brien's jovial tone did nothing to smooth him down. The solicitor paused and then went on in a more reasonable tone, 'Can you tell me honestly, either of you, that anything you have heard so far is likely to persuade the court of her innocence?'

That was a facer, because there was only one honest answer. 'All the same,' said Maitland and was aware as he spoke of the feebleness of the argument, 'I do feel there is a case for further investigation.'

'I told you so,' said O'Brien complacently. 'Look here Mr Shaw,' he went on, in a tone not calculated to soothe ruffled feelings, 'why don't you talk to Mrs Johnstone alone? Ask her straight out what she wants to do? I guarantee her instructions will be to let Maitland go ahead.'

'But in that case – ' Antony felt a certain sympathy for the solicitor. 'The Harleys have been my clients and my firm's clients for years. I can't . . . I've got to give them what they want.'

'Then you're going to find yourself in a quandary,' O'Brien pointed out. 'There isn't a counsel in England will accept instructions to plead against his client's wishes.'

It was only too clear that David Shaw understood this well enough. He put down the half-empty glass of juice and got to his feet. 'I shall take the first opportunity of speaking to her,' he said stiffly. 'After that – ' A gesture completed the sentence and he turned and left them without any further farewell.

Maitland who had been quietly concentrating on his drink, put down the glass and turned to his companion. 'What next?' he asked.

'I imagine our dear Kate will engage a new solicitor,' said O'Brien. There was more than a trace of complacency in his tone. 'In the meantime, we proceed as planned. What are you going to do first?'

'I'd like to make a start this afternoon with Mrs Johnstone's maid and Dr Trevelyan's nurse,' said Maitland thoughtfully. 'Always supposing I can find them, of course. Do you want to come along?'

O'Brien had a grin for that. 'Do you really want me?' he asked. 'It's sometimes easier – '

'I know, I know. We can compare notes tomorrow.'

'But you aren't going to stop there?'

'No, there are the Harleys too; and then the Charles Johnstones, of course, and the Lambs. In the course of talking to them – in so far as they are willing to talk – I may get wind of some further friends and acquaintances. That should do to be going on with, don't you think?'

'It should indeed. You might tell me now, what decided you?'

Maitland had a grimace for that. 'If I *had* made up my mind, things would be much simpler,' he admitted.

'But you *are* wondering,' said O'Brien shrewdly. 'And they're on your conscience now, like or not.'

'I suppose they are.' The other man sounded rueful. 'And since it has been a hell of a morning,' he added, draining his glass and looking around for the waiter. 'I vote we have another drink before we go into the dining-room.'

IV

Daisy, the lady's maid, had a certain righteousness of her own that made Maitland despair from a very early point in their interview of calling her as a witness to refute, in some small measure, the testimony of the other servants. That was after he had run the gauntlet of the parlourmaid's eyes on his arrival. O'Brien had told him that the Johnstones' house was kept fully staffed, which struck him as odd because surely, even if Kate were freed, she wouldn't wish to return there. However, in this case it was convenient, and eventually he was allowed to talk to Daisy in the library.

She was friendly enough, and obviously, in her rather unbending way, fond of her mistress. She didn't like the other servants, and was glad to lay the blame for any domestic skirmishing there might have been squarely on Douglas's shoulders. But when it came to the one point where she might have helped – the question of what Kate had been doing in her husband's room on the afternoon of his death – she stiffened up at once at the suggestion, though it was worded as tactfully as he could manage, that she might in any way have been guilty of a dereliction of duty.

'Madam had asked me to look after his things,' she said. 'And so of course I did so, and I'm sure she never had cause to think otherwise. Buttons off his shirts indeed, as if I would allow such a thing! But I don't know why he couldn't employ a man of his own like any normal person.'

So he asked her about the day of the murder, but all she would admit was having seen Dr Collingwood's back as he went down the stairs from the first to the ground floor. She had been just coming out of Mrs Johnstone's bedroom and she couldn't say, not on oath she couldn't, whether the doctor had been in the master's room or not. As for the other visitors in the house that day, she hadn't seen hide nor hair of them.

So he gave it up, and Daisy herself showed him out. He was glad enough not to have to encounter Sophie, the parlourmaid, again; though in other circumstances, of course, he would have been glad of the opportunity of questioning her. The slight mist that had further depressed his spirits that morning, had turned now into sunshine. The walk round the corner to Cheston Place, where Dr Trevelyan both lived and practised, was all too short.

He recognised the house at once, even before he checked the number, from the annex that James Collingwood had mentioned. There was no surgery that afternoon, he found Dr Trevelyan's receptionist busy with her records. Her name, Richard Kells had told him, was Amy Hunter; he thought she looked a nice girl, and was surprised at the show of anger with which she greeted his careful explanation of his presence. 'Dr Trevelyan is the most careful man,' she told him. 'The morphine couldn't possibly have gone missing in the ordinary way.'

'You're saying somebody took it deliberately?' Antony asked her, and hoped the blunt question would have at least the merit of making her think. But she answered without hesitation:

'Well, of course!'

'Who had the opportunity?'

'Need we look any further than Dr Collingwood?'

'That's what I'm here for. For instance, Dr Trevelyan would have had an even better opportunity, wouldn't he?'

'The drugs are kept in his room, certainly,' she admitted frigidly. 'But Dr Trevelyan would never –'

'I'm not saying he would have done, you know, only that he could have. What about the patients?'

'The cupboard is locked, I don't see how any of them could have got it open.'

'Let's explore the idea a little. Where is the key of the cupboard kept?'

'In the top centre drawer of Dr Trevelyan's desk.'

'And he doesn't spend a great deal of time in his surgery does he?'

'Well, no.'

'So that one of Dr Collingwood's patients, or even someone from outside, might have slipped past you without your seeing.'

In spite of herself she was growing interested now. 'Not someone from outside,' she objected. 'I don't see how they would have known where to look.'

'But someone could have slipped by you.'

'Yes, I'm always pretty busy. There's a notice in the waiting room asking patients to report to me when they arrive, but unless they do I might not see them.'

'One of Dr Collingwood's patients then?'

'The same thing would apply to them, they wouldn't know where to look.'

'Yes, I see,' Maitland was thoughtful. 'But if somebody on Dr Trevelyan's list . . . this opens up a whole new idea, you know.'

But he had said too much. She was alarmed now, fearful that she had been indiscreet. 'I don't know what idea you've got into your head,' she said sulkily, 'but I can't help you any further.'

'Thank you, Miss Hunter, there's no need.' He was as eager to be gone as she was to see the back of him, and he couldn't altogether hide it.

'You ought to talk to Dr Trevelyan,' she said, relenting a little.

'I can't at this stage, not until I see him in court. I'm for the defence, as I explained to you, and he's a witness for the prosecution.'

'Oh, so he is,' she said blankly, obviously not understanding a word of the explanation. But they parted a few moments later on good enough terms, and he walked down the street towards Grosvenor Place with his mind buzzing with conjecture.

In spite of the briefness of these two interviews it was already four o'clock. He weighed the advantages of going

68

back to chambers, but decided that the walk home would clear his head and he could phone from there to see if there was anything that needed his immediate attention. But when he got to Kempenfeldt Square he forgot all about that. Gibbs was hovering in the hall, as was his habit, with the information that Mrs Maitland had gone out; and while they were speaking Vera came out of the study looking a little anxious, which surprised him. 'There's a lady here to see you, Antony,' she told him. 'I thought as Jenny was out I'd better keep her company till you arrived.'

'We were not expecting you so early, Mr Maitland,' said Gibbs. The implication was clear enough that somewhere, somehow, there had been a dereliction of duty. Gibbs was a disagreeable old man, who refused to be retired, and now that he seemed to approve of the new Lady Harding they had all despaired of his ever doing so. Antony acknowledged the thrust with an absent-minded smile. 'Who on earth is it?' he asked, turning to Vera.

'Mrs Collingwood,' said Vera. 'Your Dr Collingwood's mother.' She came a little closer to him and lowered her voice. 'She's in great distress, Antony. If you'd like me to sit in on the interview – '

'Thank you.' There was no doubt that his gratitude was heartfelt. 'It will be like old times,' he added, following her across the hall and through the open door of the study.

This was Sir Nicholas's favourite room, the one that was normally in use except when there was entertaining to be done, or when Vera's complicated and expensive stereo equipment was providing a concert in the drawing-room. Vera went in, saying in a rallying tone, 'Here he is, Mrs Collingwood.' And Maitland, following, saw at once the reason for her hearty manner. Mrs Collingwood, huddled by the fire in the chair that was usually Sir Nicholas's, was probably at no time a particularly cheerful looking woman. Today she had obviously taken no pains with her appearance, and though her coat was neat enough her hair straggled and she held

69

a handkerchief to her nose, sniffing occasionally, in a way that made Antony very thankful indeed for another woman's presence. When the visitor gave him her hand, it lay limply in his for a moment and she looked up at him, her eyes swimming in tears. He disengaged himself, and went to stand on the hearthrug with his back to the fire. Vera left the other armchair for him, in case he cared to use it later, and seated herself on the sofa.

'Well now,' said Maitland, and realised as he spoke that he was echoing the encouragement in Vera's tone. 'What can I do for you, Mrs Collingwood?'

She blew her nose before she answered. A damp woman, he thought, and it was perhaps reprehensible that much of the sympathy he would normally have felt for her was cancelled out by this reflection. 'It's about James,' she said.

'I thought it might be,' he told her gravely. 'I saw him yesterday you know. He's in good shape, good spirits.' But in all honesty he qualified that after a moment. 'All things considered,' he said.

'Richard told me that too.' In spite of the reassurance she sounded almost resentful. 'He can't be anything but uncomfortable in that place, but Richard says there's nothing to be done about it until the trial. And even then, he says . . . Mr Maitland, what do you think of James's chances?'

'You must realise it's early days yet. I've seen him and heard his story, I've seen Mrs Johnstone – '

She came erect at that, the handkerchief for the moment forgotten. 'That woman!' she said, and again he was surprised by the venom with which she spoke.

'Do you know her?'

'Of course I don't.' Now she was scornful. 'But I've had to listen to James go on and on about her, and about the children. Women like that, not content with a husband of their own – '

'I think, you know,' – he glanced at Vera as though for inspiration – 'that there was some genuine affection there.'

70

'And what right had she to feel affection for him I'd like to know? When he might have found himself a good wife long before this.'

'Mrs Collingwood, what are you trying to tell me?'

'That it's all her fault. If James has done what he shouldn't – '

'You feel Mrs Johnstone misled him?'

'I am saying that's obvious.'

'Those are not my instructions.' He thought she might demand an explanation for that, but she was too taken up with her own troubles. 'Your son is pleading Not Guilty, you know,' he told her.

'You're supposed to be on his side, Mr Maitland. The best way to defend him is to make it quite clear that that women seduced him.'

He sat down then so as to meet her gaze more squarely. The tears were gone now, she gave him an angry look. 'Those are not my instructions,' he said again. And again she did not query the remark.

'What are you going to say for him then? Richard told me it would be a joint defence.'

'In effect it will be. Each of the defendants will have his own counsel.' He set the record straight automatically, though he doubted that she understood the implications of what was said.

'I don't think that's good enough,' she told him flatly.

This time his glance at Vera was anguished, and to his relief she decided to take pity on him. 'You could help us if you would, Mrs Collingwood,' she said. Mrs Collingwood turned on her almost fiercely.

'Us?' she queried, and now there was no doubting the belligerence of her tone.

'Lady Harding is a barrister herself, a former colleague,' Antony explained. To his surprise and relief their visitor seemed momentarily to have forgotten her distress.

'What do you mean, help?' she asked suspiciously. But

that was infinitely preferable to the tearful atmosphere that had preceded it.

'Always helpful,' said Vera, reverting to her elliptical style, 'to know something about a client's background.'

'Well I can tell you that.' She actually went so far as to tuck her handkerchief away in her handbag. 'Always a good boy he was, right from being little. Not like some boys, cruel. Not that I approve of everything they taught him in medical school, mind you, but it wouldn't have changed his nature as much as that.'

Maitland, being to some extent absolved of responsibility for the interview, which he did not think would be the slightest use in the long run, began to see some humour in the situation. 'I can quite see that it wouldn't,' he said. There was a solemnity in his tone that made Vera glance at him sharply, but Mrs Collingwood seemed perfectly satisfied with the response.

She seemed to have got the bit between her teeth now. 'Always a good provider, my Joseph was,' she said. 'James was set on this doctoring business right from the beginning and Joseph was determined he was going to go through with it. Went to a good school, James did, and then up to Leeds which they say is as good a place as any. And, like I said, just as kind and considerate a boy as he always was. Of course, we would have liked to see him buy into a practice when he graduated but my poor Joseph died just about then, so there was no question of it. James insisted I buy an annuity, he wouldn't be happy unless he knew I was looked after. He got a good job, or said he did, and was always ready to help out when I was a bit short.'

'Certain you're right about the kind of person he is,' said Vera. What was not clear to Antony was how she could know anything at all about his client's character, but perhaps the remark was merely intended to be a palliative. 'I think it would help you, you know, if you could bring yourself to believe in him.'

Mrs Collingwood seemed more bewildered now than anything else. She looked from one of them to the other, and then said shaking her head, 'But Richard told me – '

'What did Mr Kells tell you?' asked Maitland, when it became apparent that she wasn't going to continue.

'He said he daren't tell me to hope too much.'

'To an extent he's right.' Maitland's tone was gentle now, which was unwise, as Vera could have told him. 'I don't think he meant to imply that your son is guilty, though.'

The handkerchief was out again. 'You have been a great comfort to me, Lady Harding,' said Mrs Collingwood, which Antony considered both inaccurate and unfair. He thought it was time to bring her attention back to himself. 'What do you know about Richard Kells?' he asked.

'He's been a good friend of James's on and off almost all their lives. But I've not seen him for several years until he came down to Tilham to tell me about – about what had happened to James.'

'Did he explain the position? That your son was charged jointly with Mrs Johnstone.'

'Yes he did. That's why I thought – ' She turned to look at Vera, anxious again for sympathy. '*You* understand, Lady Harding; you would have felt just the same way.'

'Did he seem to know the Johnstones?'

'He said he had met her once when he was dining with James and she was having dinner at another table with a woman friend. I think they joined forces and all sat at the same table. But I didn't want to hear about her, Mr Maitland' – the handkerchief was in full play again – 'because it was quite clear to me that she was up to no good.'

At this point Vera seemed to realise that any interest that Maitland might originally have felt had dissipated now; also perhaps that he was a little at a loss as to how to close the conversation. She took over, therefore, gently leading Mrs Collingwood back to reminiscences of her son's younger days. Even so it was quite half an hour before the woman

73

left them. Antony accompanied her into the hall, and closed
the front door behind her with a sigh of relief. When he got
back to the study again Vera was mending the fire. She
turned and smiled at him, but her words had their customary
gruffness. 'Don't understand you,' she said. 'What's all this
about Richard Kells?'

'He's my instructing solicitor,' said Antony. He did not
sound as if he was giving the matter his full attention.

'All the more reason – '

'He's a friend of Collingwood's. Presumably he has visited
him and knows the set up of the Trevelyan household.'

Vera considered that. 'Don't think much of the idea,' she
said at last.

'Well, I don't myself, but I'm pretty desperate for ideas
at the moment. With a man like Douglas Johnstone, I
shouldn't be surprised at all sorts of motives cropping up.
But opportunity is quite another matter.'

'What sort of a man?' asked Vera. Her questions had the
habit of being very much to the point.

'Hard, puritanical, a successful businessman.' Maitland
waved a hand vaguely, as if this by no means constituted a
full list of the dead man's attributes. 'But I've barely scratched
the surface yet, Vera. Give me time.'

'When will the trial come on?'

'Not until the Hilary term, I dare say.'

'Gives you plenty of time.'

'Unfortunately there's not too much to be done. All the
people who might have helped us are being called by the
prosecution.'

'All of them?'

'No, I'm exaggerating, of course. I did have a sort of idea
while I was talking to Dr Trevelyan's receptionist, but it
seemed to evaporate while I was walking home.'

'Bad luck.' That, from Vera, was the equivalent of the
most eloquently expressed sympathy.

'Anyway you saved my life and I'm grateful.' He might

74

have said more but at that moment they heard the sound of voices from the hall. Gibbs lurking again, of course, but Antony recognised also his wife's clearer tone. 'I'd better go,' he said. 'Uncle Nick has heard about as much about the case as is good for him for the time being.' He exchanged a grin with Vera and went out.

V

Meg and Roger Farrell were perhaps the Maitlands' closest friends. They had known Meg – better known to the theatre-going public as Margaret Hamilton – by far the longer, ever since she had first come to London to make her name by a particularly ferocious portrayal of Lady Macbeth. But circumstances had thrown Antony and Roger into an intimacy that was welcome to both of them, and it was Farrell's habit on a good many evenings a week to call in on the Maitlands after dinner and after he had regretfully escorted his wife to the theatre. In general, this formed a pleasant contrast to the day's affairs, but on this particular evening Maitland was awaiting his friend's arrival with some eagerness. Roger was a stockbroker, and there might be some things to be learned concerning the dead man's affairs of which Antony's instructing solicitor was not aware.

The opening night of Meg's new play had been only a week ago, but neither of the Maitlands had seen it yet. Roger was inclined to be querulous as he accepted a cup of coffee. 'It looks set fair for a long run,' he said. To his eyes, Meg's popularity was not an unmixed blessing.

'Never mind,' said Jenny sympathetically. Antony who was pouring brandy tilted the bottle a little further.

'I did warn you,' he said. 'And you had a whole week at Grunning's Hole before she started rehearsing, so you shouldn't grumble.'

'That's all very well – ' But Roger was never one to hold

75

on to a grievance. 'I don't think she's altogether happy in the part, though,' he added.

'Well, be that as it may' – Antony completed his errand of mercy and went to take his usual place on the hearthrug – 'there's something I think you can help me with. I want to pick your brains.'

'You might wait until he has at least caught his breath after all those stairs,' said Jenny. At which the two men exchanged a glance, because Roger, as usual, was in something like the peak of condition, and the remark could only be regarded as pure provocation.

'I'll wait if you like,' said Maitland generously.

'If ever there was a chap for raising one's curiosity – '

'All right, so I go ahead. It's very simple really, what do you know of a firm called Johnstone and Lamb?'

'You've got yourself mixed up in the Johnstone murder case,' Roger asserted.

'You've heard about that?'

'I could hardly help it. It's one of the main topics of conversation in the City. If you want to know about the firm, they are extremely competent, extremely successful. Very well thought of.'

Antony grinned. 'So I understand. But O'Brien was so cynical about them that I think he must have been bitten some time. Not by that particular firm, of course.'

'Their record *has* been rather spectacular,' said Roger thoughtfully.

'Tell me about Johnstone then.'

'Good Lord, I don't know anything about him. Only what the whole world knows.'

Maitland moved away from the fire and after an indecisive moment seated himself. 'And what might that be?' he asked idly. Neither of his hearers was at all deceived by this assumption of casualness. Roger sipped his cognac. 'The Johnstones were always a moneyed family,' he said after a moment. 'The brother, Charles, is with Bramley's Bank; not just a bank

76

manager I mean, not even in the advance department, but one of the joint general managers.'

'Yes I heard that, but it's Douglas I'm asking you about.'

'He was said to be a hard man – '

'Now where have I heard that before?'

' – and he certainly had principles of the most rigid sort. And if you're going to say "All the better", I can only tell you he wasn't popular. There were some injustices where the staff were concerned. Or so I've heard.'

'Now you do interest me. What sort of injustices?'

'If anything went wrong someone had to take the blame. You may say that's fair enough, but rumour has it that Douglas himself was not always without fault. There was a chap called Glidding, he was dismissed for a mistake he always maintained was made by Douglas Johnstone himself. Personally, I believe him, but that's only my opinion. I may be wrong.'

'Glidding,' said Antony, rather as if he were trying to find some particular significance in the name. 'Don't you know anything more about him than that?'

'No, just his name.'

Maitland was searching his pockets again. The envelope was produced first, but when Roger obligingly passed across a propelling pencil he shook his head. 'Always break the things,' he said, and produced his own stub of pencil in triumph. 'Glidding,' he said again, writing. 'But how the hell could a stockbroker's clerk get hold of morphine?'

'I should think it very unlikely myself,' said Roger. 'This is interesting, though, isn't your client guilty?'

'Haven't you learned by now,' said Jenny, teasing, 'that all his clients are innocent?'

'Not all.' Maitland seemed to take this statement with undue seriousness. 'In this case, however, . . . well, look here, Roger, I've got to find out what I can about Johnstone and his associates.'

'Well, I don't know of any other employee with a grievance

77

but I do remember that some of the oldest members of the Exchange shook their heads when Glidding got the sack, and said it wasn't the first time something like that happened.'

'Lamb then. Ernest Lamb. What does that remind me of?'

'Toytown,' said Jenny promptly. 'Ernest the policeman and Larry the Lamb.'

'I knew there was something. Well, Roger, what about it?'

'I know Lamb personally, if that's what you mean, though not well. He is a different kettle of fish altogether, a much more pleasant person. Meg and I have dined with them from time to time.'

'Then you can tell me . . . if you call him a pleasant person you mean I suppose that the words "first murderer" don't immediately spring to mind?'

'I mean exactly that. Look here, Antony, I thought that this case was exactly what it seemed, a domestic matter.'

'Sordid,' said Jenny. 'Uncle Nick doesn't like it one little bit.'

'And Mrs Lamb?' Antony had no intention of being distracted from his questions.

'Jean?'

'That's right. She was actually in the house on the day of the murder.'

'Sinister in the extreme,' said Roger, with a tinge of sarcasm in his tone. 'Jean is the gentlest soul alive.'

'If her husband had a motive, she might be under his thumb.'

Roger was smiling. 'Not that either. She's . . . oh, well, I suppose you could say she's her own woman.'

'And what exactly do you mean by that?'

'It's perfectly obvious,' said Jenny. 'She has a mind of her own.'

Antony had a dissatisfied look. 'This isn't getting us anywhere,' he said. 'I was hoping – '

'I've told you before, we're a peaceful lot in the City,' said Roger placidly. And suddenly Antony was on his feet again. 'You do know something,' he said accusingly.

'Don't get your hopes up. It's nothing material, nothing you could use. But there has been this rumour, a very persistent rumour, that something big is brewing and that Johnstone and Lamb are in the thick of it.'

'For heaven's sake, can't you be more specific than that?'

'That's as far as it goes. I'll ask around, of course, but I can't promise anything in the nature of startling revelations,' Roger told him.

'Never mind.' He bent to pick up the envelope and stuck it back in his pocket, glanced round to see if any glasses needed attention, and then seated himself again. 'I shall ask Meg about Jean Lamb,' he decided. 'She has been called by the prosecution and she may be a dangerous witness.'

'Why is that? She isn't . . . no, look here, Antony – '

Antony ignored the rather querulous tone of this remark. 'Because she sounds the sort of woman to be easily confused in court. I gather she's well disposed towards Kate Johnstone, but that may not do us much good.'

'Who will be cross-examining her?' asked Jenny, settling herself more comfortably now that she sensed the business part of the evening was over.

'I'm not talking about cross-examination. But Garfield's prosecuting – '

'The solicitor-general?'

'He is now. The trouble is – you've probably heard me say this before – he's the sort of chap who'll most likely take evidence of misconduct to be evidence of guilt of murder. And as he is a persuasive chap he should be able to persuade the jury to take the same view. As a matter of fact, I think this is one case where we ought to do as they do in the States, and spend a week over jury selection.'

'What makes you say that?' asked Roger, interested.

'Kevin O'Brien, who is defending Kate Johnstone – and

who incidentally, got me into this mess – is what they call a colourful figure; the court will probably regard the pair of us as a couple of disreputable fellows, and see our clients in that light too.' He moved his shoulders as he spoke, as though throwing off a burden, and said briskly. 'That's about enough of that for one evening. Let's talk about something else.'

VI

Although it was late when Roger left them to fetch Meg from the theatre, Antony went to the telephone and dialled the number Richard Kells had given him. 'I've got a name for you,' he said without apology when the other man identified himself. 'Glidding. I don't know the Christian name. He was a clerk with Johnstone and Lamb until eighteen months ago and left under something of a cloud. He blamed Johnstone for his dismissal. There could be something in it.'

'What do you want me to do?'

'I expect you have your own favourite firm of enquiry agents. Cobbold's are good, if you haven't. Find out anything you can about him. Anything at all.'

'All right, I'll do that. I've a bit of news for you though, Mr Maitland, that may not please you too much.'

'This is a fine time of night for bad news.'

'It's just that the date of the trial has been put forward. They'll be bringing it on in this session, probably just before the Christmas adjournment.'

Maitland swore, briefly and to the point. 'But I don't really see that it makes much difference,' he said, after reflection. 'I'm not very hopeful about any pre-trial enquiries I may make. Will you set up a conference for Sunday, anywhere that's most convenient for O'Brien.'

'Do you want to see James again?'

'Not for the moment. If you come round to chambers, about eleven-thirty tomorrow morning, I'll put you in the picture as to what has happened today. Can you do that?'

'I'll be there. Good night.' Kells rang off so abruptly it almost seemed as though he did not wish, or could not bear, to hear an more. Antony turned from the phone to find that Jenny had cleared cups and glasses and was kneeling on the hearthrug poking the remains of the fire into a blaze.

'You *are* worried Antony,' she said, when she saw she had his attention. 'Was Uncle Nick right after all?'

'Nothing like that. It's just . . . if only people weren't so damned trusting, love.'

'There's nothing to be done about that,' said Jenny sadly, wishing she could offer him more comfort. But then she brightened. 'I think I shall get you another drink. Things may look better after that.'

'And dirty another glass? Heaven forbid. Anyway it's past our bedtime,' he said, and held out a hand to pull her to her feet.

FRIDAY, 19th NOVEMBER

The next day, and the Friday, were devoted to all the thousand and one details that needed attention in chambers. He barely saw Sir Nicholas, who was struggling with a brief, and consequently unapproachable; but he took time to wonder how Vera was coping with her husband in this mood. There was always, with a difficult case, a point at which Sir Nicholas reached what his nephew called 'the snarling stage'.

Meanwhile, Willett had been set on, and ordered on pain of his life to be tactful, to make various appointments for Maitland on Saturday. Willett, as has already been indicated, was the one of the clerks over whom old Mr Mallory presided who most nearly identified himself with Maitland's interests. He was reputed never to walk when he could run, and indeed always seemed to be in a hurry, but Maitland had long since ceased worrying about his competence. For all the air of frenzy about his activities, he never seemed to forget any serious matter.

Antony arrived home rather late on Friday, having been delayed by a conference that couldn't possibly be arranged at any other time. At the last moment he found that his uncle was still in his room, and they shared a taxi back to Kempenfeldt Square, but Sir Nicholas was still preoccupied and did not again comment on his nephew's connection with the Johnstone case.

When he got upstairs to his own quarters Jenny was waiting for him in the hall. 'There's a man,' she said, gesturing rather distractedly towards the closed door of the living-room. 'He must have been very insistent, or Gibbs wouldn't have sent him up.'

'What's wrong?' asked her husband, correctly interpreting this.

Jenny shook her head in a bewildered way. 'He's a seedy little man,' she said, at which her husband's eyebrows shot up, because from Jenny this was the extreme of uncharitableness. 'I can't think,' she went on, 'why he wants to see you.'

'Then I'd better do something about finding out.' Maitland took two quick strides across the hall and flung open the door of the living-room. Jenny made no move to follow, so he closed the door carefully behind him and paused a moment to take stock of his visitor.

He thought immediately that the word 'seedy', however unlikely it was that Jenny should have used it, fitted the man to admiration. A thin man, of medium height, in an off-the-peg suit that had seen better days. That was at first glance. A second look assured him that there was more to it than that. A pair of very bright blue eyes met his with a look that was almost challenging. But there was something else – he sought for the word – something predatory about the man. He took a moment to savour the word and then smiled to himself over its extravagance. Perhaps it was no more than the result of a beak of a nose and a thin face.

'Are you Mr Maitland?' the stranger asked abruptly, without any other attempt at a formal greeting.

'I am.' Maitland crossed the room until he and his visitor shared the hearthrug. 'You'd better sit down,' he said, gesturing, 'and tell me what all this is about.'

The newcomer obeyed, insofar as he perched himself on the edge of the wing chair that had its back to the window. 'The Mr Maitland who is defending Dr James Collingwood?' he said insistently.

'The same. Do you know something about the case?'

That seemed to amuse the stranger. 'Do I?' he said, and emitted a hoarse bark of laughter.

'In the event, I shall be glad of your help.'

'It's not so much help I'm offering.' He was more sure of himself now. 'I've got something that will blow your defence sky high.'

Maitland took a moment to look him over. 'It seems very unlikely that you can know anything at all about the defence,' he said coldly.

'What I don't know I can guess, can't I? Too much of a lady to admit to taking a tumble, isn't she? And him too much of a gentlemen to embarrass her by admitting what they'd been up to.'

'Are you by any chance talking about the two defendants in the Johnstone case?'

'Yes, I am. That's how I see them anyway.' Antony didn't think he had ever seen anyone leer before, but that was undoubtedly a good description of the look the stranger gave him. He turned deliberately, went to his uncle's chair and seated himself.

'You're going to tell me you were in the employ of the late Douglas Johnstone,' he said.

'Now that's right smart of you, Mr Maitland. I was.'

'Am I to be permitted to know your name?' That was very much in Sir Nicholas's manner, but as usual Antony was quite unconscious of it.

'David Bingham. My friends call me Dave.'

'I hardly feel I can aspire to those heights. What is it that you have to tell me, Mr Bingham?'

'It's not so much what I can do for you as what you can do for me, Mr Maitland. It's the other side that has the money, Mrs Johnstone and her lot.'

'You want paying for your information?' He was blatantly stalling for time, because this was something he didn't like the look of at all.

'Now we're getting down to it.' Bingham's tone held a certain satisfaction. 'It's not so much paying for the information I want, as paying to keep my mouth shut.'

'I see.' If he displayed his rising anger he might never know the unsavoury details of what this man had to say. 'You'd better tell me what you have to sell,' he said carefully, but couldn't quite keep the scorn out of his voice.

'I did tell you. My silence.'

'Until I know what you are proposing to keep silent about – ' Maitland's voice was harsh, but he did not attempt to finish the sentence. The other man eyed him with the first shade of uneasiness evident in his manner, but even so he was prepared to be explicit.

'I can give the police precise details of an afternoon those two spent together at a small hotel,' he said. 'One that isn't too particular about that kind of thing.'

'How do you know the police haven't this information already?'

'I know the clerk on the desk, see. Nobody's been around asking him questions. He's the one that would have to identify them, because naturally it was a false name that was used.'

'Are you proposing that we square the clerk too.'

'Don't worry, I was tactful with him. He hasn't an idea who the visitors were, but if there was an identity parade, for instance – '

'I see.' And indeed he did, only too clearly. 'May I ask why you have come to me instead of to Mrs Johnstone's lawyer?'

'People in my line of business get to know all you chaps. O'Brien has got a temper, I've heard about that.'

For the matter, Maitland had a temper himself, and at that moment might have been described as hanging on to it with both hands. 'You thought perhaps that I should receive you more graciously?' he asked, with some irony in his tone.

'Well, there's things been said about you from time to time, Mr. Maitland. So I thought if you was to explain to him – '

'You took my agreement for granted?'

85

'Wasn't I right?' His confidence had returned now, and somehow the smug way he said that proved the last straw.

Maitland came to his feet in a hurry. 'You can take your information to hell for all I care,' he said, in a blaze of anger.

For a moment it seemed that Bingham did not take that in, though he cowered a little in his chair. 'I'll go straight to the police,' he warned.

Antony reached out his left hand, took the visitor by his lapels and jerked him to his feet. He resisted the temptation to shake his unwelcome visitor as a terrier might shake a rat and said with surprising amiability, 'That will save me the bother of communicating with them myself.'

For a moment Bingham's only concern was to wriggle himself free, then he made for the door. When the sofa was safely between them he turned and spat out, 'It will put the lid on their case, you see if it doesn't.'

Antony made no attempt to follow him. 'They will also be interested to know of your attempt at blackmail,' he said gently. And at that the other man finally turned tail. Jenny, coming into the room a moment later, had a questioning look.

'What have you been saying to that poor little man, Antony? He looked as if all the hounds of hell were after him.'

'Has he gone?'

'Yes, he rushed out and left the door open behind him, and when I went to close it I heard him clattering down the stairs. I can't think what Gibbs will say.'

'He'll say it to Uncle Nick and not to us, and Uncle Nick is submerged in a brief at the moment.'

'Well, what did he want . . . that man?'

'To blackmail me; or rather,' he added quickly, seeing her expression, 'to blackmail one of my clients. And that reminds me, love, that I'd better phone Kevin O'Brien straight away.'

'It's that case, is it? You'd better go down and see Uncle Nick after supper. You know he's interested.'

86

'I doubt if he would listen. Or perhaps . . . there's an ethical problem, love. I might put that up to him after I've talked to O'Brien.'

O'Brien was at home. It was his wife who answered the telephone; he had married a woman from his home town and Antony felt vaguely comforted to hear the North Country accent when she answered his call. It also put an idea into his head. 'Yes, he's here,' she said, when he asked for Kevin. A moment later O'Brien's voice sounded in his ear.

Antony told him briefly what had happened. 'You ought to regard it as a compliment,' he concluded, 'that he chose to approach me rather than to come to you. Obviously I'm regarded by the more shady elements of his profession as being a bit on the shady side myself.'

'Will he go to the police?'

'I rather think not. He ran like a rabbit when I mentioned blackmail. But there's the question, you see, O'Brien; ought we to go to them ourselves?'

'Not on your life.' He paused and then added in his most persuasive tone, 'This fellow seems to have upset you, Maitland, but can't you see it's really a stroke of luck? At least if the police find out later, we're prepared for the worst that can be said in court.'

'I'm not too happy to think that both our clients lied to us.'

'Well, you knew that, didn't you?'

'I suppose I did,' said Maitland reluctantly. 'But that's not quite the same thing as having it rammed down my throat.'

'You'll feel better when you've had your dinner,' said O'Brien encouragingly.

'Well, at least . . . do you mind if I put the problem up to Uncle Nick?'

'Of course not. He,' said Kevin, preparing to replace the receiver, 'is a man of some common sense.'

So Antony and Jenny went downstairs at about half past

87

nine. 'Though I'm not at all sure,' said Antony despondently as they went, 'that he'll even listen to me.'

'Yes, you said that before. If he's as taken up with his brief as all that,' said Jenny thoughtfully, 'it will be a new experience for Vera. I wonder how she'll cope.'

She needn't have worried. They found the Hardings in the study, Sir Nicholas not at his desk as Antony had certainly expected, but seated by the fire with an inch of ash already on his cigar. He greeted them in his usual leisurely way and got up to do the honours. There was Benedictine for Jenny, his best brandy for Antony (which was in itself an argument for coming down after dinner); Vera, who had developed a gentlemanly taste in drink since her marriage to Sir Nicholas, was already supplied with cognac.

'How's the Connor brief coming along, Uncle Nick?' asked Antony, as Jenny and he seated themselves side by side on the sofa opposite the fire.

'Coming along, coming along.' Sir Nicholas, back in his chair again, was as vague as though he had never heard of the matter before.

'I was afraid you might be working on it.'

'Time enough for that in chambers,' said Sir Nicholas with a nonchalance that took his nephew's breath away. This was the second miracle that Vera had worked, the first being in getting the servants to accept her, but this was even more startling; in the past you had taken your life into your hands when Sir Nicholas was in the throes of a difficult brief. Now, thought Antony irreverently, a child could play with him. He looked at his new aunt with some respect.

'You're looking weary, Antony,' Sir Nicholas remarked after a moment. 'The Collingwood case, I suppose. Can't you leave your work behind in chambers, as I do?'

'Only since you married Vera, Uncle Nick,' Jenny pointed out. It was a matter of principle with her never to let him get away with a remark that she considered unfair. 'But you're quite right, it is the Collingwood case. A man came here before dinner – '

'So Gibbs informed me. Not a desirable character, Sir Nicholas,' he mimicked, though he had not Antony's facility in that gentle art, 'but very insistent that he should wait for Mr Maitland. So as Lady Harding was in the study – '

'That's the chap.' For the second time Maitland recounted his talk with the man called Bingham. 'O'Brien thinks there's no obligation for us to inform the police,' he said when he had finished, and his uncle seemed to have no immediate comment to make. 'I said I'd put it up to you.'

Sir Nicholas sat up straight at that and lost the ash from his cigar. 'This is carrying your scruples a little too far, Antony,' he said. 'Of course you have no obligation to say anything at all.'

'In that case, I have to agree with O'Brien that his visit was a blessing in disguise. At least, we know the worst.'

'And the fact that your client is untrustworthy does not bother you at all?' asked Sir Nicholas coldly.

'I knew he wasn't altogether truthful, I told you that, Uncle Nick. Heaven and earth, I should probably lie myself in his place.'

That was an unfortunate remark, because it reminded his uncle of one or two episodes in the past that were best forgotten. He was winding himself up for speech when Vera, with a warning look at the younger couple, said tranquilly, 'I think Nicholas is in the right of it, Antony. If your mind is at rest now, there's no need to talk shop any more.' Which was pretty cool, as they agreed later, when shop was one of the favourite topics of conversation in that intensely legal household, and Vera herself one of the worst offenders. But meanwhile, Sir Nicholas had been silenced, a thing Antony would have been glad enough to have the trick of, and they spent a peaceful evening talking of other things.

SATURDAY, 20th NOVEMBER

I

The first interview that Willett had fixed for him was for eleven o'clock the following morning with Kate's parents, Horace and Amelia Harley, and it couldn't be said that Maitland was looking forward to it with any degree of pleasure. Wilgrave Square has always been elegant, and those few houses that still remain in private hands are mostly extremely well cared for. The Harleys' house, on the north side – a more desirable situation, on the whole, than the south side, where the Douglas Johnstones had lived – was no exception. Antony hesitated a moment before he went up the six steps to the front door. He knew he should have his thoughts in better order by now, but he still hadn't decided how best to conduct the interview. Besides, he was expecting to be admitted by something, or somebody he should have said, as ill-disposed as Gibbs or Sophie, and he wasn't looking forward to that either.

However, the door was opened to him by a cheerful middle-aged woman, with curly grey hair escaping from beneath a conventional maid's cap. She didn't actually address him as Dear or Dearie, but he felt it was touch and go. Perhaps he had been similarly mistaken about her employers. 'Mr Harley said to put you in the study,' she told him, and proceeded to do so.

Though there wasn't a speck of dust anywhere, it was obviously a room that was never used. A measure of their opinion of me, he thought rather drearily, as counsel for the man who seduced their daughter. They would have a preconceived notion of him, as they had of his client, and plead he never so eloquently he did not see how he was going to change that.

They came in together, a comfortable, kindly looking couple, Horace Harley no taller than his daughter and his wife Amelia probably something under five feet. It was a moment before he realised that each of them was favouring him with a frosty look, and when Harley spoke his voice was no more welcoming. 'I agreed to see you, Mr Maitland, for one purpose only,' he said. 'To get an explanation of this conspiracy.'

Whatever greeting he had been expecting, it was not that. 'Conspiracy?' said Antony blankly, and his bewilderment was genuine. He glanced at Mrs Harley as he spoke, but if anything she liked him even less than her husband did.

'I should hardly have thought it needed any explanation,' she said.

'Well, it does.' Perhaps it was as well he hadn't thought out carefully how to conduct the interview, all this would certainly have put him off his stroke.

Mrs Harley moved serenely past him to seat herself. 'This may take some time,' she said. 'I think perhaps, Horace – '

'Certainly.' He indicated a chair. 'If you will sit down, Mr Maitland – '

Antony obeyed, though as usual, when anything troubled him, he would have welcomed the relief of movement. 'You'll have to believe I don't understand what you're talking about,' he said bluntly.

'Will it help if I tell you that I have spoken to David Shaw since your interview with my daughter on Wednesday last?'

Well, of course, that was only to be expected, and Horace Harley was obviously a man accustomed to getting his own way. 'It doesn't explain the use of the word "conspiracy",' said Antony, and sounded, he thought, as disagreeable as either of the Harleys.

'Kathleen has completely rejected our advice, so much so that David is no longer her solicitor. It seems that you and

91

this man O'Brien between you persuaded her . . . and if that isn't conspiracy, Mr Maitland, I don't know what is.'

'Your daughter, along with my client, James Collingwood, wishes to plead Not Guilty, Mr Harley. I don't see anything wrong with that.'

'Can you honestly say that you think that is the best course for her? Can you persuade the jury that what she says is true?'

'I can't give you a positive answer to either of those things.'

'If the court could be persuaded that she was acting under this man Collingwood's influence – '

'Yes, but I don't believe that, you see.'

'Are you so convinced of her innocence then?'

That was a difficult question. If it had been asked of O'Brien he thought his colleague would have found the answer an easy one, and again he envied him his assurance. 'I think she has the right to plead as she likes, and to have a fair trial on the evidence,' he said carefully. 'We shall try, O'Brien and I, and our respective juniors, and of course our instructing solicitors, to see that she gets one. My part is to see that all the evidence is . . . well, available. And that's why I need your help.'

Horace Harley had a contemptuous look for that. 'You may be condemning her to life imprisonment instead of a short sentence,' he pointed out. 'If the court could be persuaded that she was acting under Collingwood's influence . . . but I suppose it's all advertising for you.'

Considering Antony's hatred of publicity, that remark might well have annoyed him. Instead he looked from one to the other of them, spread his hands in a somehow helpless gesture, and said, 'You think your daughter is guilty. Persuade me.'

It was Mrs Harley who took up the challenge. 'We know Kathleen, Mr Maitland. She was always wild and headstrong, even as a child.'

'Perhaps you can give me some examples of that.'

'When she was ten years old she refused to go any more to the temple.'

He tried not to let his bewilderment show. 'The temple?' he echoed, in as matter-of-fact a tone as he could assume.

'Where we worship. The preacher is such a wonderful man, Mr Maitland.' For a moment it seemed that she had forgotten the purpose of the interview and was bent on converting him to her own religious preference. 'We have a place in the country too, and Kathleen was always asking us to go down there, but it was really that she wanted to get out of going to the temple here.'

'You let her have her own way about that?'

'Of course not, that was quite out of the question. She continued to accompany us until she was married. But I think you can see now why we were so relieved when a sensible man like Douglas Johnstone proposed to her and she accepted him.'

'That was her own wish? No persuasion necessary?'

'Entirely her own wish. We should not have dreamed of coercing her.'

In view of what she had just told him, that seemed an extraordinary statement, but his expression remained as solemn as that of either of the Harleys. 'What was your opinion of Johnstone?' he asked.

'A fine man. Not conventionally religious,' (did she consider her own views orthodox?) 'but with very fine principles.'

'We both thought she would be safe with him,' said Horace Harley. He spoke in a heavy tone as though the thought of how wrong they had been oppressed him.

'How long was it before you realised that all was not well with them?'

'Unfortunately, not long. It was Kathleen's headstrongness, you see, she would have her own way about everything. You couldn't expect Douglas to put up with that.'

93

'You felt some resentment towards him then, because Kate's life was not all you could have hoped for her?'

'I'm not quite sure what you mean by that, Mr Maitland.' Harley again took a hand in the proceedings. 'If you are implying – '

Maitland's interest was aroused and he genuinely had not thought how the question might sound. 'There was no hidden meaning in my remark,' he said and essayed a smile.

'In any event, the answer is No. What blame there was attached to Kathleen, not to Douglas.'

'And that's all the reason you have for thinking her guilty? It's a far cry from being – what did you say? – headstrong, to killing your husband.'

'Of course we don't think she would have done such a thing left to herself. That's why we blame this man Collingwood so much. *Your* client,' Amelia Harley reminded him.

'Precisely. My outlook is bound to be rather different from yours . . . don't you think? For instance, what do you know of him?'

'That he insinuated himself into the house when Dr Trevelyan was busy, and without Douglas's knowledge. That he persuaded Kathleen into an irregular relationship. That she had asked Douglas for a divorce.'

'Who is your source of information there?'

'Douglas himself. And I might say I quite agree with his desire to keep the children after Kathleen had behaved so badly.'

'Had Kate spoken to you about Dr Collingwood at all.'

'She may have mentioned his name, but that was before we knew what was going on.'

'You don't think that a man of Douglas Johnstone's rather stern character – forgive me, you don't altogether agree with me about that, do you? – might have made some enemies outside his immediate domestic circle?'

'I know of nobody,' said Horace Harley, but he glanced at his wife as though for confirmation.

She shook her head vigorously. 'I am sure there was nobody,' she said. 'In any case there is the question of the morphine. It's obvious that your Dr Collingwood supplied it.'

'In many families there is somebody who has died of cancer, for instance, for which such a thing might have been prescribed, never finished, never thrown away. It is by no means certain the stuff came from Doctor Trevelyan's surgery.' Maitland said that firmly enough, but to himself he admitted some doubts.

Mrs Harley seemed to consider that. 'I'm a little disappointed in Dr Trevelyan,' she said, after a while.

'You know him then?'

'Certainly we do. He attends us when necessary, but that isn't often I'm glad to say.'

'And why are you disappointed in him?'

'Because he is obviously uneasy about the provenance of the morphine,' said Horace Harley, coming back into the conversation. 'He is being called by the prosecution, which shows what *they* think about it, but he still persists in his liking for Collingwood, and in doing his best to defend him.'

'After all,' Maitland pointed out mildly, 'he knows him a good deal better than any of us do.'

'That's hardly the point,' said Mrs Harley, in a tone that meant, 'That is enough of that subject.' 'Well, you have heard something of our side of the affair, Mr Maitland. Do you still think it right to encourage Kathleen to defy us?'

'It isn't exactly a case of defying,' he said, feeling for the right, the most persuasive words. 'I think she deserves a fair hearing, that's all.'

'Then there is no more to be said.'

'But I haven't ... I hoped – '

Perhaps Horace Harley had some human weaknesses after all, such as curiosity. 'I think we should hear what Mr Maitland has to say,' he suggested.

His wife inclined her head. Maitland who thought her

95

decidedly the more formidable of the two, addressed himself this time directly to Horace Harley. 'I was wondering what you can tell me about the Charles Johnstones,' he said.

Evidently here were two other people of whom his hosts did not approve. 'They have the guardianship of the children,' said Mrs Harley bitterly.

'But surely – ?'

'We would have taken them. Naturally they should have come to us. They will learn bad habits in that house.'

'Charles doesn't share his brother's admirable nature then?' asked Maitland, and was rewarded by a sharp glance from Amelia.

Horace said only, 'A frivolous pair,' and that seemed to be the end of that subject.

Antony raised his final point without much hope. 'Douglas Johnstone's business partner?' he said, and made the words a question.

Mrs Harley sniffed. 'I know nothing against him,' she said, and he couldn't help the feeling that this was a disappointment to her. 'But Jean, now. I always thought Jean would be a good influence on Kathleen.'

'Have you changed your mind about that?'

'Not exactly. But Kathleen could have used some guidance, Mr Maitland, and she wouldn't listen to us.'

Maitland came slowly to his feet. 'When did you last see your daughter?' he asked.

'Fully a month ago, wasn't it, Horace?'

'And Douglas Johnstone?'

'At the same time. They came here to dinner.' She got up too and her tone was as final as she could make it. 'I had hoped to make you realise that what you are doing is no kindness to Kathleen, Mr Maitland,' she said coldly. And though some conventional words of farewell were uttered, the coldness persisted until he got himself out of the house.

The trouble was, he thought, as he looked around for a taxi, that for all he knew she might be in the right of it. He tried to console himself with the thought that Kate Johnstone was O'Brien's problem, not his. But all the time he was uncomfortably aware of having taken on, tacitly at least, responsibilities towards both the accused.

II

Because it was Saturday he went back to Kempenfeldt Square for lunch, which he and Jenny had always taken with Sir Nicholas on that day. Unlikely as it seemed, Sir Nicholas appeared to have forgotten temporarily his own troublesome brief. He was full of questions about Antony's activities that morning, and though his only comment was, 'Sheer waste of time,' it was evident that he was not any too pleased with what he heard. Vera, however, to Antony's amusement, obviously enjoyed the discussion; so much so that he wondered, if, after all, she was missing her own practice at the bar. Jenny occupied herself with her lunch. Always a better listener than a talker, she was today perhaps unusually silent, but he hoped that the only reason for this was that she was missing his company on a day when she might normally have expected to have him with her.

His next expedition took him in the opposite direction to the one that morning. The Charles Johnstones lived in Bayswater, an old house, not quite so spruce as the one the Harleys occupied, and again many in the vicinity had been converted into flats, or places of business. Charles Johnstone was a big, shaggy man, improbably attired, presumably in honour of the weekend, in an equally shaggy suit of tweeds. He must have been waiting for the visitor, for he met him in the hall himself, and took him immediately into a large, comfortable drawing-room.

His wife, Felicity, was waiting for them and it occurred to Antony that, in her husband's clothes (which would have fitted her very well) and with the addition of a bristling moustache, one of the couple might very well have passed on a dark night for the other. But they received him affably, even effusively, which after his experience that morning with the Harleys was a welcome change. 'Not that I can quite see what we can do,' said Charles, when he was finally convinced that his guest did not wish to accept any of the rather staggering variety of refreshments he offered, 'beyond standing by and looking after the children. But, of course, if you think – '

'I am . . . fishing in the dark,' said Maitland. He had used that phrase before and found it a useful one to reassure a nervous witness. Not that either of the Johnstones appeared in the least bit nervous; excited would have been a better word, but subduing that excitement because of the seriousness of the occasion.

'Well then!' Charles Johnstone suddenly became businesslike. 'This matter of poor Douglas – '

'You understand I'm not acting directly for your sister-in-law. My client is Dr Collingwood.'

'What of it? Comes to the same thing,' said Charles cheerfully. Antony took a moment to wonder how he had reached that conclusion.

'I'd like you to begin by telling me about your visit to your brother's house that day.'

'Well now, it's no secret that Douglas and I weren't all that good friends. Nothing wrong, you understand, just that we had nothing in common. So that luncheon invitation was by way of being a formality, and Felicity was glad enough to have a good excuse. When I got there and found Douglas hadn't turned up either I thought it was a bit thick. But I must say I enjoyed my lunch in Kate's company all the more for it, and I don't think my wife will blame me for that.'

Felicity Johnstone smiled. 'You had the children as chaperons,' she pointed out.

'Not all the time.' It was obvious there was some joke between them about this, and Anthony thought, looking from

98

one to the other, that here if ever there was, was a truly united couple.

'Then you can tell me about Kate, that day.' He did not apologise again for the use of the Christian name, he thought they would understand well enough that he did it to avoid confusion. 'Was there anything about her manner – ?'

For the first time Charles Johnstone frowned. 'If you're thinking of getting us to say anything against Kate – '

'Believe me, that was the furthest thing from my intention.'

Luckily both of them seemed to take his sincerity on that point for granted. It was Felicity who broke the little silence. 'I wish now I'd gone. I know Kate rather better than Charles does, you see. I used to go there often to see the children. We haven't any of our own, and they're such darlings. But Charles can tell you – '

'She was just as she always is, quite herself.' That was said a little too vehemently.

Maitland said, apparently at random, 'You must understand, Mr Johnstone, that the truth is the best weapon the defence can have. Even if it is unpleasant.'

'Nothing unpleasant,' said Charles hurriedly. 'I thought, if you must have it, that she seemed rather sad that day. Of course, she had been worried about Dougie, it was his first day up and he was rather pale and quiet. Kate is a good mother, you have to give her that.'

Antony turned to look at Felicity. 'Didn't she ever confide in you, Mrs Johnstone?'

'If you mean about this Dr Collingwood, no she never did. Only, looking back, I think she probably dragged his name into the conversation sometimes when it wasn't necessary, and that might have been just for the pleasure of talking about him. But you can tell Kate – will you be seeing her, Mr Maitland? – that the children are quite all right with us.'

'And a darn side better off than ever they were with Douglas around,' said Charles explosively.

99

'If Kate . . . of course, we can't adopt them legally while she is alive, but we can get legal guardianship. Tell her that, Mr Maitland,' Felicity urged. For the first time he thought she had a worried look; perhaps it was concern for her sister-in-law, perhaps for her husband's unguarded tongue.

'I certainly will. I wonder, Mrs Johnstone, whether you would allow me to see the children before I go.'

'I don't see why not, do you Charles?'

'No objection in the world.' Charles was hearty again. 'Meanwhile, we'd better get on with the inquisition, hadn't we? Are you casting me in the role of First Murderer?'

That was an odd question, an echo of his talk with Roger. 'Does that mean' – he looked from one to the other of them – 'that you don't believe Kate is guilty?'

'You've been talking to Horace and Amelia,' Felicity Johnstone asserted. 'They never could see any good in Kate, not from the time she was a child.'

'You've known them so long?'

'Oh yes, for many years.'

'Anyway, Mr Johnstone, about your question, I'm not casting anybody for that role at present. But I should like to know if you noticed anything when you went up to your brother's room after lunch.'

'I wasn't looking for anything out of the ordinary,' Charles said. He seemed a little put out that the question should have been asked. 'I knew about the injections, of course, and I dare say if the hypodermic hadn't been there I'd have noticed it, but as it was everything was as usual.'

'Do you know Dr Trevelyan?'

'All my life,' said Charles, and, 'Ever since we were married,' said Felicity, almost in one breath.

'A reliable type?'

'Careful,' said Charles, nodding his head.

'But I'm not so sure he's at his best with children now,' said Felicity.

'And your brother's partner?'

100

'Oh, Ernest is the salt of the earth. But if you're looking for somebody who was really close to Kate, Mr Maitland, why don't you talk to Jean?'

'She's a prosecution witness,' said Antony, not elaborating. He hesitated; these two seemed well disposed, so why not put the question? 'I wonder, Mr Johnstone, if you could tell me anything about your brother's will.'

'Well yes, as it happens, I do know its terms. Everything to Kate, so you can't make a motive for anybody else out of that. I suppose if she's convicted the children will inherit, but that is up to the lawyers.'

'Would Kate be competent to take over her husband's share of the firm?'

'That wouldn't arise. There's a clause giving Ernest the option of buying in Douglas's shares, and he told me he was going to exercise it. Of course there's some delay in the circumstances, but I gather there's some sort of an agreement being worked out that covers him whatever happens.'

'I see.' And that, indeed was food for thought. 'The children now,' he said, and smiled at Felicity Johnstone. 'Would it be convenient – ?'

'I'll get Helen to bring them down.'

'Is that the same nursemaid they've always had?' Maitland asked.

'Yes, we wanted to make as little upset for them as possible.'

'Then perhaps you could fetch them yourself, Mrs Johnstone. She's another person I'm not supposed to talk to.'

There was a little delay before the children were ushered in. From their neat appearance Maitland concluded that the time had been spent in tidying them up. Dougie, as befitted his seniority, came forward first to shake hands, and very grown-up he was about it. Janet held back a little, surveying the stranger, but after a few moments she decided he was harmless and came forward in her turn. They were an attractive pair, but for the moment Antony's interest was caught by

101

Mrs Johnstone's proprietorial air. It was obvious that, however she viewed her sister-in-law's arrest, some good had come out of the whole tragic business for her.

Afterwards he was to think it strange that neither of the Johnstones had thought to caution him to be careful while talking to the children. He hoped it was because they instinctively trusted his common sense. But after a moment when Janet, whom he quickly realised was the natural leader, overcame her shyness and said to him, 'Aunt Felicity says you've been to see Mummy,' he realised that perhaps this frankness was the most sensible policy the Johnstones could have adopted.

He was seated again now and the little girl came to stand beside his knee. She was as dark as her mother, pretty enough now and probably going to be a beauty. Dougie was fairer, a stolid looking little boy for all the talk there had been of his delicacy. It obviously wasn't lack of interest that kept him more silent than his sister, he followed their exchange with almost painful anxiety. 'Yes,' said Maitland, 'I saw your mother on Wednesday. She was very well and sent her love to you.' For once in his life a slight distortion of truth did not give him even a moment's discomfort.

'Aunt Felicity says she can't come and see us because people are saying bad things about her,' said Janet confidingly.

'I'm afraid that's true, but we're doing our best to put it right.'

'And our doctor?'

'Dr Collingwood?' He essayed an enquiring look at Mrs Johnstone, who nodded vigorously.

'Yes, that's right,' she said, 'they're very fond of him.'

'We love him,' said Janet firmly, putting the record straight. 'Don't we, Dougie?'

Dougie, more cautious, or perhaps more inhibited, contented himself with nodding his head. Janet taking a firm hold of Maitland's sleeve said confidingly, 'I think I shall trust you.'

That was probably the last thing he wanted to hear. 'You can trust me to do my best,' he said, and hated the phrase as he used it. But he caught Dougie's eyes just then and was surprised by a sympathetic, almost conspiratorial look, as though to say 'These women!' 'Do you remember the day before you came to live here with your aunt and uncle?'

'The day Daddy went to heaven,' said Janet not meeting his eyes now. But Dougie was growing more courageous.

'The day he died,' he said baldly.

'That's right. What did you do that day?'

'Dougie had been ill.' Janet was obviously not altogether in sympathy with this invalidism. 'But it was a lovely day because Mummy was in to lunch and Uncle Charles came. We usually have lunch in the nursery.'

'Dr Collingwood came to see you in the afternoon?'

'He came to see me,' said Dougie importantly.

'Were you surprised to see him?'

'Oh no, he usually comes when one of us is ill. Of course Dougie wasn't ill any more, just taking care,' said Janet in a very grown-up way.

'Did either of you go downstairs with him when he left? Or did your nurse do so?'

'Not exactly,' said Janet. 'Dougie was tired, but I went halfway down the stairs with him.'

'That is, the stairs between the nursery floor and the one where the bedrooms are?'

'Yes, of course.' Janet was never patient with explanations. 'But I was sorry he was going so soon, you know, so I stood and watched him.'

'Could you see the head of the main staircase from where you stood?'

She obviously thought this a silly question and said again, impatiently, 'Yes, of course.'

'Did he stop for any reason?'

'No, why should he? He went straight across and down the stairs and I expect Mummy had asked Jean to bring the tea.'

Maitland was careful to keep all emotion out of his voice. An interesting point but not really material. The prosecution were not maintaining that James Collingwood had filled the hypodermic himself. All the same he was glad he had seen the children, and when the farewells had been made, with due gravity on Dougie's part and a good deal of enthusiasm on Janet's, he watched them go out in Felicity Johnstone's wake with an uncomfortable realisation of what it must mean to their mother to be separated from them as well as from everything else that makes life worth living.

The offers of refreshment were renewed, it was a little time before he could get away, but he managed it at last and went out into the still, sunny afternoon. Just one more interview before he could call it a day. He hoped he would find Ernest Lamb as congenial as the Johnstones.

III

The Lambs had chosen to live in one of the big new blocks of luxury apartments overlooking the river. The furnishings looked new too, as though they had decided to make a clean sweep of all their old possessions. To Maitland's eye, accustomed as he was to the rather shabby elegance of his uncle's house, this looked odd; but he soon realised that Jean Lamb, in spite of Danish furniture and curtains with a decidedly modernistic pattern, must be regarded as a homebody. Everything was arranged for comfort, the colours she had chosen matched the season's flowers to perfection. It was not until later that he thought that it was perhaps a rather sterile comfort, no newspapers lying about, no open books on the sofa, no hi-fi equipment, and an electric fire with simulated logs.

Willett had obviously made the arrangements well, and taken care of any necessary explanations. It would have been embarrassing to turn Mrs Lamb from her own fireside, but throughout his time in the flat Maitland saw no trace that she was at home. The first thing he thought, as Ernest Lamb got up to greet him, was that a description he had been given of Jean would have fitted her husband well enough. Gentle, sympathetic, a chap you could talk to. Lamb had none of Charles Johnstone's effusiveness, he was smallish and slightly built with straight, almost black hair and a neat black moustache. But the aura of kindliness, to Maitland's perhaps too imaginative eye, surrounded him like a cloud.

'You're acting for Dr Collingwood,' he said. From another man this might have sounded like an accusation, but from him it was a simple statement of fact. 'And I gather from Mr Kells, who spoke to me before your clerk phoned to make this appointment, that you are also co-operating in Kate's defence. Though I admit I didn't understand perfectly what he meant by that.'

Maitland, who had taken the chair to which his host had waved him, set himself to explain the position in as few words as possible. When he had finished, 'That won't please Horace and Amelia,' said Lamb shrewdly.

'You know the Harleys?'

'Oh yes, we're old friends. But I have to admit they're a little set in their ways, won't change their minds either about anything or anybody once they have made them up.'

Maitland smiled at that, he couldn't help it. 'I gathered as much as I met them this morning,' he said.

Ernest Lamb was continuing with his own train of thought. 'I've known Kate almost since she was a baby,' he said, 'and that's why I'm glad you're helping her.'

'I'm doing my best,' said Antony. It was the second time

that day he had used a form of words he particularly disliked, but the circumstances in this case seemed to warrant it. He hesitated, and then went on. 'There's a little difficulty here, Mr Lamb. I want to know what you think about the Johnstone household – the Douglas Johnstones I mean – but I have to ask you only to tell me what you know of your own knowledge.'

'No hearsay,' said Lamb obligingly. He did not, to Antony's relief, ask for any explanation of the conventions by which his visitor was bound. 'I think all their friends knew that there were difficulties between them. Douglas was an irritable chap, I always put it down to his illness myself, and though I think Kate tried hard to please him she wasn't always very successful.'

'Were any of the disagreements about the children?'

'I shouldn't be surprised if that was the case. But they were always tucked away out of sight when I was in the house, Mr Maitland.'

'Do you think Kate was hard enough pushed to have considered murder?'

'No, I don't. But your client now' – he smiled as he spoke as though to rob the words of any sting they might have – 'I don't know him well enough to be sure.'

Well, that was one thing he knew now, if Collingwood had acted it had been with Kate's connivance. If only he had some of O'Brien's certainty . . . but he hadn't, so the best thing seemed to be to ignore the remark. 'You've heard the gossip?' he asked, and Lamb looked up quickly, perhaps surprised by the roughness of his tone.

'Gossip? Oh, yes, I didn't take any account of it.'

'You spoke just now as though you knew Dr Collingwood, at least slightly.'

'He attended Jean once when she had 'flu. Dr Trevelyan was down with it at the same time.'

'And Dr Trevelyan' – it was Maitland's turn to smile – 'is another old friend?'

'Most certainly he is.'

'When did you last see the Johnstones?' He seemed to be jumping from subject to subject, a practice Uncle Nick would have condemned, but for some reason he was finding it difficult to concentrate his mind.

'About a week before Douglas died, I should think. Jean . . . but that's part of the forbidden subject, isn't it, Mr Maitland?'

'I'm afraid it is.' His tone was rueful. 'What can you tell me about a man called Glidding?' he asked.

'You've heard about that. Now I wonder – ' Lamb's tone was thoughtful but he did not attempt to complete the sentence. 'I wouldn't have been so hard on the man myself, his indiscretion was doubtful at best; but Douglas insisted, and in the circumstances there was nothing I could do. I do wonder how you heard about it though.'

'I understand there was a good deal of talk on the Exchange,' said Antony non-commitally. 'Do you think Glidding would bear any malice?'

'I'm sure he would, but not to the extent of murder. For that matter, I don't know whether he would realise which of us was responsible. Are you telling me I too ought to be on my guard?'

'I hardly think so. I take it you never had any wish yourself to dissolve the partnership.'

'Douglas was a very able man, Mr Maitland. I couldn't have wished for anyone better. A partnership with him was certainly to my advantage.'

'But now I understand you are taking over the firm altogether, when all the formalities are completed.'

'Who told you that?' He answered his own question a moment later. 'Charles, I suppose. He's the most indiscreet man I know, but no harm in him, no harm at all.'

'But, in this instance, was he right?'

'The situation is complicated, but, yes, substantially he was right.'

107

'I see.' His tone too was thoughtful, and after a moment Lamb said in a sharper voice than he had used before:

'If you want the whole story, as things are at present it will probably be to my advantage.' Then he smiled, good-humoured again. 'But if you're looking for a motive for murder, Mr Maitland, there's one you may not already have considered. Felicity and Charles have been longing for children ever since they were married, and from what Felicity tells Jean it's pretty hopeless. They are both mad about Dougie and Janet, and naturally they would get the guardian-ship.'

'That's a little too complicated for me,' said Maitland lightly, though in fact he had been thinking of little else since he saw Felicity Johnstone with the children. 'Unless Kate was accused and then convicted . . . and how could anybody ensure that?'

'It wasn't a serious suggestion, they are friends of ours,' said Ernest. 'What I think I was trying to get over to you, Mr Maitland, was that it's nonsense looking for motives among our own close circle of acquaintances.'

'You've made your point.' Maitland got his feet. 'Though you wouldn't accept my suggestion concerning Glidding either,' he reminded his host. He paused for a moment, and then added, 'You say you welcome my interference. How do you suggest I proceed?'

'I can quite see your difficulty.' Ernest Lamb was worried now. 'Nobody but a fool would suggest accident, but I can't believe . . . never mind, I wish you well, Mr Maitland, even if I do think you're going to make a fool of yourself if you try to bring this murder home to Charles.'

Antony was moving towards the door. 'We seem to have got our wires crossed somewhere,' he said, as amiably as his host might have done. And again he used the trite phrase that was meant as reassurance. 'I'm fishing in the dark, that's all.'

IV

'That's a couple of bright kids,' he told Jenny that evening. They had just got back from the theatre where Meg's new play, *The Potter's Vessel,* as Roger had so dolefully predicted, showed every sign of becoming a howling success. Jenny was all set for a discussion of the evening's entertainment and had turned on the electric fire in the bedroom while they had a nightcap. But Antony's mind, as soon as the performance had ended, had reverted inexorably to the day's events; she sensed his mood and set herself to listen.

'From what you told me before, you got rather more from them than you did from their aunt and uncle,' she said.

'You could say that. But it doesn't help, you know. The prosecution aren't building their case that way, and O'Brien doesn't need convincing.'

'You mean he realises, anyway, that Dr Collingwood couldn't have done it without Kate?'

'Not exactly. He's made one of his acts of faith, love, and I wish I could do the same thing.'

That silenced Jenny for a moment. She knew well enough how her husband was made, a man incapable of passing by on the other side. If there were the slightest doubt . . . that was the trouble, it worked both ways. 'You've got some idea in your head, Antony,' she said at last in a small, almost apologetic voice.

'You know I always have ideas, it doesn't mean anything. But I do think I might talk to Sykes tomorrow.'

'What on earth could Inspector Sykes do for you?'

'Chief Inspector,' he corrected her automatically, as he had been doing ever since the detective was promoted, though he knew by now that it wasn't the slightest use. 'He isn't on the case so there's no impropriety in my talking to him. But he might be persuaded to tell me – '

109

'What?' asked Jenny, when it became apparent that he had gone as far as he intended. But Antony only shook his head at her, and sipped his drink, and presently she began to talk about the play.

SUNDAY, 21st NOVEMBER

I

They breakfasted late the next morning, and as the sun had evidently decided it was too much to expect that it should shine two days in succession in November, it wasn't too much of a penance to give up their usual walk after the meal had been cleared away. Antony made for the telephone, which lived on the writing-table in the corner, and prepared for some fast talking. The questions he was about to ask were indefensible, and though he had given a good deal of thought to the subject he had not yet made up his mind how to make them sound anything else.

Chief Detective Inspector Sykes of the Criminal Investigation Department at Scotland Yard (Bill to his friends, though Antony had it on good authority that his given name was Marmaduke) was the one member of the force with whom Maitland came close to being on terms of friendship. Because of certain incidents in the past, the detective chose to regard himself as being in some way beholden to him. A strict sense of fairness should have led Maitland to admit that any such debt had long since been repaid, in fact in his own mind he was perfectly well aware of this; all the same, he was not above playing on the delusion when it suited him. So that now he did not scruple to telephone Sykes at home; on a summer's morning he wouldn't have a hope catching him indoors, Sykes was a keen gardener. But on a dull morning at this time of year, with everything tidied away for the winter, he was most likely to be found by his fireside with the more staid of the Sunday papers.

And, sure enough, Mrs Sykes produced him without any

111

delay. There was never any mistaking Sykes's comfortable north country accent, nor the fact that his encounters with Maitland generally afforded him some amusement; to which latter fact Antony had long since resigned himself. The amusement was very evident after the first greetings had been exchanged, which took a little time as the detective was a man very particular about the proprieties. 'I haven't heard anything of you for at least a month, Mr Maitland,' he said.

What had happened a month ago was something he preferred to forget, though he doubted if he ever would. At any other time he would have resented the reminder, but this morning his mind was concentrated exclusively on his clients, and he let the thrust pass without comment. 'You see,' he said confidingly, 'I want to pick your brains.'

There was a pause while Sykes thought that out. He never reacted quickly, always with due deliberation. 'I've heard that you and Mr O'Brien are teaming up together,' he said at last.

'Our clients' affairs seem to call for a certain amount of co-operation,' said Antony cautiously. 'And you're quite right, it is the Johnstone–Collingwood affair I want to talk to you about.'

'Nay, I'd nowt to do wi' that,' said Sykes, lapsing, as he sometimes did, into the dialect of his youth.

'I know that. Strange as it may seem, I have read my brief,' said Maitland, with some pride in the achievement. 'But don't tell me you don't know anything about the case, because I wouldn't believe you.'

Sykes ignored this. 'Inspector Conway now – ' he said, deliberately tantalising.

'You know perfectly well – ' That was a trap into which he wasn't going to fall. 'It's only a very small piece of information that I want,' he added persuasively.

'Are you telling me your instructing solicitor hasn't been provided with all he's entitled to.'

'Nothing like that. This has nothing to do with the case

112

against Mrs Johnsone and Dr Collingwood,' Maitland told him.

'Then I don't quite see – '

'Just something I'm curious about.'

That brought another pause. Antony thought he could follow the other man's train of thought well enough. A joint defence means they're pleading not guilty, and with Maitland involved that probably means the defence are looking for someone else to take the blame. 'I don't think I can help you, Mr Maitland,' said Sykes regretfully.

'No harm in hearing the question, is there?'

'So long as you understand – '

'This is something the police must know, unless Conway's work was incredibly sloppy, which I doubt. But it has nothing to do with the present indictment, so I dare say the prosecution has never even heard of it. There's someone else who has a very good motive, at least as far as I can make out.'

'I knew it,' said Sykes, with something like a groan.

'I'm talking about Douglas Johnstone's business partner, Ernest Lamb. Was his alibi investigated?' Sykes made no immediate reply, so after a moment Antony went on, 'There is just a chance that because the case against Kate Johnstone and James Collingwood seemed so obvious nothing was done about the other.'

'If that's the best you can come up with, Mr Maitland – '

'It doesn't sound as though you think much of the idea.'

'Well, I must say, I don't.' There was another pause (Sykes struggling with his conscience, thought Maitland irreverently). 'I don't want you making a fool of yourself when the case comes on, Mr Maitland,' the detective said at last.

'On the whole I should prefer not to myself.' If he thought there was a general conspiracy to take a gloomy view of his coming performance, this wasn't the time to say so. 'Besides – you know me pretty well by now, Chief Inspector – I've never attacked anybody in court unless I felt pretty sure in my own mind that I was right to do so.'

113

'I know that, so you'd better forget this one. Conway and Mayhew went through his whole day, minute by minute. He hadn't a chance of getting anywhere near the Johnstones' house, let alone getting in unobserved and changing the stuff in the hypo.'

'So Conway did wonder,' said Maitland thoughtfully.

'He's a careful man, Mr Maitland, you have to give him credit for that. And from what I hear' – from anybody else the reminder might have sounded malicious – 'you've got a difficult one on your hands this time.'

'Well, I'm grateful for your help. There is just one other thing – '

'I might have known it,' said Sykes, but now the amusement was back in his voice again. 'Somebody else with a good motive?'

'Nothing like that. The enquiries that were made into the provenance of the morphine.'

'I can't help you there. The prosecution's case is that it came from Dr Trevelyan's surgery.'

Maitland did not point out that he knew that well enough already. There might be an opening there, but not until they got into court. He was clear enough in his own mind that the receptionist knew nothing of what might have happened. 'I won't keep you any longer then,' he said. 'And I mean it, Chief Inspector, when I tell you I'm more grateful than I can say.'

But he did not attempt to hide his disappointment from Jenny, who was waiting to hear the results of this very irregular conversation. 'And all it's done is make things more difficult for you,' she commiserated with him, when he had finished. But he knew well enough that he hadn't really expected anything else.

II

The conference had been called for early afternoon in chambers, where Maitland had commandeered his uncle's room. 'A jolly sight more comfortable than we would have been at my place,' said O'Brien appreciatively, wandering about before the others arrived. Even so, when the full complement of lawyers was there they found the conditions a little crowded. Kevin had brought along his junior, Joseph Whitehead, the son of the man with whom Antony had done his pupilage many years before. Derek Stringer, a colleague in chambers, who was also acting as Maitland's junior, was also there; Richard Kells, of course; and Kate Johnstone's new solicitor, Geoffrey Horton.

Maitland was a little uneasy about this last choice, though he had himself mentioned Horton's name to O'Brien among others. Geoffrey was an old friend, who had often briefed him in the past, but it was also true that there had been a clash of personality between them on more than one occasion. So that now Antony was not at all sure how the combination of himself and Kevin O'Brien would strike the solicitor.

And when all was said and done it was an abortive meeting, with no conclusions reached.

Only both Kells and Horton had been advised that the parlourmaid had slightly revised her evidence; she now remembered seeing Dr Collingwood hand Mrs Johnstone a package on the afternoon of Douglas Johnstone's death. They would both take the first opportunity of asking for their clients' explanations, but however specious these might be it wasn't exactly a matter that was pleasing to the defence.

The date of the trial was discussed – 'before Christmas, anyway,' said Kells, not looking very happy about it – and another day was set for joint consultation, a little nearer to

115

the time when they must go into court. Antony reported briefly on the interviews he had conducted, and reflected a little ruefully that if Horton had been instructing him instead of Kells he would have heard something about that once the meeting was over. As it was, Geoffrey left with the others after about an hour. Only Kevin O'Brien lingered behind, as though he had something further to say.

At first, however, he made no attempt to open a conversation, strolling across to the window and looking down into the court below. Antony waited with what patience he could muster, and after a while Kevin turned back to the room again. 'It wasn't quite a complete report, was it?' he asked.

'Not quite complete,' Maitland agreed, not attempting to elaborate.

Kevin moved back towards the fireplace again. 'We'll get on a whole lot better if you'll be frank with me,' he said in a voice that seemed studiedly calm. And then, 'Damn it all, man, that's the whole point of the exercise, isn't it?'

'Two things,' said Maitland, not attempting either to argue or to justify himself. 'There seemed no reason to bring them up in the general meeting. When I went to see the Charles Johnstones, I talked to the children.'

'You didn't mention that.'

'No, because . . . A six-year-old and an eight-year-old. How much credence would be given to their evidence? But I believe Janet, she's the younger of the two, when she says she watched James Collingwood go downstairs after he had visited Dougie that afternoon. He went down the two flights to the hall, without lingering on the bedroom floor at all.'

'Yes, I see your point. That's more or less what the prosecution are contending, isn't it?' If O'Brien had been irritated before, all trace had left his manner now, perhaps because he seemed to be getting his own way. He said with a smile, that showed more appreciation than might have been expected for Maitland's feelings, 'Has it helped to convince you of your client's innocence?'

116

'I'd give a good deal for a good solid belief in either of them.'

Kevin looked astonished. 'I thought – '

'You thought I was a peculiarly credulous individual.' He laughed when he saw the other man's expression. 'No, I'm not getting at you, I just wish I was as strong-minded as you are, that's all.'

O'Brien thought that over for a moment, before he decided that, if no compliment was exactly intended, no slight was meant either. 'Two things, you said,' he remarked.

'This is something that really shouldn't go any further, even among our colleagues. I had a word with Sykes – '

'He wasn't on the case.'

'That, if you think about it, is precisely the point. After a certain amount of skirmishing he told me we needn't bother to go after Ernest Lamb. Conway went into his alibi and it's as solid as a rock.'

'You wouldn't,' said O'Brien – and now he, like Sykes earlier in the day, was definitely amused – 'consider clearing our clients without implicating anyone else?'

'If we can't do any better, I'd settle for a Not Guilty verdict. But you know that would always leave doubts in many people's minds.'

'Is there anything else you want to follow up?'

'Not immediately. Kells is getting this chap Glidding investigated, but I think I agree with Ernest Lamb about that, there's nothing to it. Eighteen months is a long time to hold a grudge strong enough to lead to murder.'

'There have been cases.'

'Now you're going all literary on me.' He turned to depress the fire with his foot so that it could burn itself out safely after they had gone. 'Anyway, Kells has that in hand. How do you get on with Horton? He's one of the best, that's why I suggested him.'

O'Brien followed him out to the hall. 'Besides, I know he's worked with you before.'

'And may therefore be expected to bear with me. It might work just the opposite way, you know.' Maitland paused to let his companion catch up with him. 'You know, O'Brien, I wish I didn't have so high a regard for Chief Inspector Conway's thoroughness.'

'That sounds as though you're coming around to my way of thinking.'

'Y-yes.' He was obviously doubtful. 'I don't see my way,' he said after a moment.

It seemed that this time Kevin realised he was genuinely uneasy. He said briskly, 'Do what we can in court then. Collingwood will still have cause to be grateful to you.'

'That isn't quite the point.' He shrugged, and then began to move towards the outer door again. 'It may come to that, but you see I have a feeling – '

He did not elaborate on that and neither did O'Brien question him as to his meaning. They went out into the murky afternoon together and did not, before they parted, make any further reference to the case.

III

Tea on Sunday afternoon, with Roger and Meg Farrell as guests as well as Sir Nicholas and Vera, though not long established as traditions go, was rapidly becoming a hard and fast rule. Later the Hardings would be going to a concert and coming home to a late supper (an innovation in Sir Nicholas's household that Jenny could hardly believe had taken place), while the Farrells, with Meg rejoicing in her one evening's freedom, would stay on for dinner and the endless talk that goes on between close friends.

When Maitland came in they were all already assembled. The first cups of tea had been poured, and Roger, whose rather piratical appearance was belied by an unexpected streak of domesticity, had disappeared in search of more hot water. Antony gave them a general greeting and crossed to his favourite place on the hearthrug; Jenny, watching, was only too well aware that his shoulder was paining him, and had a few hard thoughts about Kevin O'Brien, who had embroiled him in a case that was proving tiresome. Sir Nicholas, probably just as well aware of his nephew's weariness, asked pertinently, 'Did your conference get you anywhere?'

'Do they ever?' asked Antony, with some bitterness evident in his tone. He moved across to take the cup that Jenny was holding out to him. 'And this one was particularly useless.'

To Jenny's relief Sir Nicholas did not say, I told you so, but only, reflectively, 'You and O'Brien should make a good team. It will be instructive to see you acting together.'

'As for that, he's got some maggot in his head that I'm not being frank with him,' said Maitland ruefully. 'There's nothing much we can do until we get into court, and when we do – '

He did not attempt to finish that, and after a moment's pause Vera said in her gruff way, 'Like to know what you mean.'

He smiled at her then. 'I suppose the answer to that is that I don't really know,' he said.

'No ideas?' she asked.

Jenny thought she could have told her the answer to that, and was surprised when her husband shook his head. 'None that lead anywhere,' he said. 'It's a question of opportunity, you see.'

Roger had come back in time to hear that last remark. He put the hot-water jug on the tray beside Jenny and passed the remainder of the hot-buttered toast to Sir Nicholas, who was partial to it. 'You were asking me about Ernest Lamb,' he said idly.

'I was interested in him,' Antony admitted. 'The trouble is, he has an alibi.'

'Who says so?' asked Meg.

'I wormed it out of Sykes. But it was all gone into by

119

Conway and Mayhew, and you know how thorough they are, Uncle Nick.'

Sir Nicholas was wiping butter from his fingers. 'I think in that case you can disregard Mr Lamb,' he said. 'Unless – '

Vera had only too obviously been waiting for her husband to finish speaking. As he broke off she said in a hurried way, 'Told us the wife was there that day.'

'She didn't sound that kind of person,' said Jenny. 'Not from what Mr O'Brien said, or from what you told us yourself, Antony.'

'Well, I shan't see her until we're in court, but the general consensus seems to be that she's a gentle, sympathetic soul. Anyway, she has an alibi herself – she was in the house, but never alone there – and as we've Kate Johnstone's word for that, I think we can take its accuracy for granted.'

'I wonder, darling – ' said Meg.

Antony waited a moment in case she wanted to complete the sentence, then asked, 'What's on your mind, Meg?'

'Not the alibi, of course,' said Meg, giving him her most dazzling smile. 'If you say she's got one I'm sure you must be right. But you're making her sound awfully wishy-washy; there's more to her than that.'

'In the circumstances – '

'She was there,' said Vera. 'She may have seen something.'

' – and as you will be cross-examining her, I presume,' concluded Sir Nicholas, 'it might be as well to heed Meg's warning.'

'I'll do that all right. But I don't see what she could have seen that Kate didn't. They were together the whole time she was in the house.'

'You said it was a question of opportunity,' his uncle pointed out. 'Who else comes into that category?'

'Dr Trevelyan, of course, was there that morning. I shan't see him either until we get into court,' he added, by way of explanation to Meg and Roger. 'As far as opportunity goes, you might say his is paramount, because the morphine was

120

kept in his surgery. But that is something we all seem to forget; mainly, I suppose, because there seems to be no shadow of a motive in his case.'

'Your researches don't seem to have taken you very far. I can't think why you bother,' said Sir Nicholas, a certain amount of asperity creeping into his manner. Antony, for once in his life not heeding the storm signals, replied seriously instead of letting the subject drop.

'Because I think those two deserve a break.'

'I should have found it a more compelling reason if you had said: "Because I believe them innocent," ' said Sir Nicholas coldly.

'Kevin O'Brien does.'

'If that is sufficient for you – '

'Unfortunately, no. But I do wonder about it, Uncle Nick. And then there are the children. Whether their mother is innocent or not, they deserve a better deal than they're getting. Not that the Charles Johnstones aren't kind to them,' he added.

'Unfortunately the law can take no account of innocent bystanders.'

'Don't I know it? But you've got to let me do this thing my own way, Uncle Nick. If the Not Guilty plea is the right one . . . Heaven and earth, I've even wondered whether my instructing solicitor might not be the guilty party!'

Sir Nicholas sat up straight at that, almost spilling his tea. 'This is madness,' he said. 'What possible reason – ?'

'No reason at all, that's the trouble. And no opportunity either. But I had a talk with Mrs Collingwood, James's mother. And I don't know why but one or two things he had said to her gave me an uneasy feeling.'

'If that is all you have got to go on – ' growled his uncle.

'It is.' There was a finality in his tone. He went to sit on the sofa between Vera and Jenny and looked round at the company. 'Let's talk about something else,' he suggested. 'When are you going to see *The Potter's Vessel*, Vera?'

121

MONDAY, 22nd NOVEMBER

Monday was filled with other duties, other briefs to study, other clients to see. Kells phoned to say the Johnstone case was on Mr Justice Carruthers's list, which pleased Maitland mildly, and that it would probably be the last case heard before the Michaelmas term ended, which didn't please him at all. There would be other conferences of course, at least one more interview with his client, but with so little actively to be done the delay fretted him. Which was unreasonable, because he realised perfectly well they were lucky to be getting the trial in before the new year; and there was probably not much difference, so far as publicity was concerned, in being the last case under the old dispensation rather than the first in the new Crown Courts that were due to be introduced after the vacation. Either might be expected to bring a little added interest, both from newspapers and public.

The last conference of the day was with a lay client, Mr Cook, and his solicitor Mr Bellerby. It was particularly annoying to Maitland because Cook insisted, in spite of a weight of evidence to the contrary, in expecting a happy outcome; and Mr Bellerby, that advocate of kindness to clients, was not the person to set him straight. That job fell to his counsel, and Antony felt distinctly ruffled by the time he left chambers.

He walked home, hoping in that way to exorcise his demon, but was inordinately annoyed when he let himself into the hall and found Gibbs hovering as usual near the door into the servants' quarters. It was foolish to allow it to irritate him, he ought to be used to the old man's ways by now, and things in general were certainly better since Vera had joined the household in Kempenfeldt Square. But he was tired, and the more weary because of the uncertainty that had been nagging at him all day.

'Mrs Maitland asked me to tell you to go straight upstairs when you came in,' said Gibbs, interrupting his train of thought.

One answer to that would have been, 'What does she expect me to do?' Another to ignore it. Which he was tempted to do, because Gibbs, as was usual with him, succeeded in sounding censorious; late or early, it was all the same, there was something blameworthy about it. So Maitland, managing a 'Thank you' as he reached the bottom of the stairs, felt that on the whole he had acquitted himself with dignity.

He did wonder, though, as he mounted more slowly than was his custom, why on earth Jenny had felt it necessary to leave that message.

She must have heard him coming, she was waiting in the hall upstairs. He thought as he bent to kiss her that she looked . . . not quite herself. Pale? But she never had much colour. 'Antony,' she said urgently, almost before he had time to straighten himself again, 'are you all right?'

'Puzzled, that's all. What on earth did you mean, leaving a message like that with Gibbs, love? Where did you think I'd be going?'

'Sometimes Uncle Nick – '

'Well, even if he did want to see me, where's the harm in that? He isn't likely actually to attack me, especially with Vera looking on.' His tone was gently teasing, but there was no corresponding lightening of Jenny's expression. 'So what's the matter?' he demanded.

'Oh, I don't know, Antony, I was worried that's all. I'd have phoned you, only I knew you'd say I was being stupid.'

He had taken her arm and was urging her towards the living-room. 'When did I ever say that?' he asked, amused.

'Well, I think you have said it sometimes,' said Jenny,

taking him literally. 'And I made up my mind years ago I'd never be like one of those stupid females in books, getting taken in by fake messages, things like that. And this seems so innocuous, so perhaps I'm exaggerating.'

'Take a deep breath and start again,' he advised her. Jenny's explanations had never been noted for their clarity. 'You got a letter? Somebody telephoned?'

'No, no, nothing like that.' She looked at him for a moment despairingly, as though wondering how on earth to make him understand. 'It was this package, you see.'

'*What* package?' asked Antony, with what patience he could muster.

Jenny went across to the table, which was already laid for dinner, and stood there with her back to it as though shielding something from his gaze. 'You know that new sweet shop on the corner of Avery street? Well, not really a sweet shop at all, one of those places that make very high class chocolates, the sort of things you send to your friends when you can't think what else to give them.'

'No, I can't say I've noticed it.'

'It doesn't matter, anyway. It's there. At the far end, on the same side as the hotel. And the card with the box said they were sending out samples to a few selected people, to get their name known, you see.'

She had all his attention now. 'You're saying somebody sent you an anonymous box of chocolates?' he demanded.

'The card – '

'Yes, I heard what you said.' He pulled her aside and stood glaring down at the box, still among its wrappings, that lay on the table. 'You haven't been eating the damned things?' he said.

'You know I never do.'

'No, that's right.' His anxiety assuaged, he spoke less roughly. 'Did you phone the shop, love? They would have told you – '

124

'I just thought I'd be making a fool of myself,' said Jenny, subdued.

'As if that mattered.' He pulled her towards him and gave her a quick hug. 'I expect it's too late to telephone now. Anyway, we'll be foolish together, love, and treat the things with the utmost circumspection.'

'That's what I thought,' said Jenny. And then, interest momentarily outweighing anxiety, 'Do you think there might be fingerprints?'

'We'll touch the outside of the box as little as possible, and just examine the contents,' he told her. He took the lid off carefully with the tips of his fingers as he spoke. Then he began to pick out the chocolates and examine them one by one. 'Are you thinking what I'm thinking?' he asked.

'If Uncle Nick was right and these interviews you've been having . . . it is the Johnstone case, isn't it?'

'It's the only one I'm what Uncle Nick calls meddling in at the moment.'

'But if somebody is trying to harm you . . . it seems such a roundabout way to go about it.'

'I don't know about that. We're pretty well guarded here, what with being at the top of the house and Gibbs always on the watch. And if it is the Johnstone case . . . it's ordinary people we're dealing with, love, not gangsters.'

'I know that.' She paused a moment watching him. 'There's nothing there, is there?'

'No there doesn't seem . . . wait a bit, though. This one with an almond on top.' Jenny pressed closer. 'Someone's been careless here, you can tell it's been handled.'

'It does look a bit squashed,' she agreed.

'Yes, and there's something else. It's very minute but that could be where a hypodermic was plunged in,' he said, pointing.

'Then . . . oh, Antony! I don't eat chocolates at all and you only eat marzipan.'

'A coincidence?'

'You always say you don't believe in them,' Jenny pointed out.

'I don't normally, but I don't see what else this can be. Where's that card you were talking about?'

'It's somewhere . . . here you are.'

Maitland studied it in silence for a moment. 'Not a printed card,' he said then. 'Fancy calligraphy.' He turned a puzzled face to her. 'But what the hell could anyone hope to gain by this?' he demanded.

'Do you think only one chocolate has been tampered with?'

'That's what it looks like. It seems somebody didn't care which of us got hold of it.'

'I suppose either way it would be . . . a distraction for you.'

'That's one way of putting it. Have you some more brown paper, Jenny? I'll bundle the whole thing up and drop it in on Sykes in the morning.'

'Not on Inspector Conway?'

'You know how he disapproves of me. But if what I think is there he'll hear about it soon enough.'

Jenny went off on her errand, and after a while removed a fairly neat parcel into the hall. When she came back Antony was pouring sherry. 'Don't you think you'd better go down and tell Uncle Nick first?' she said.

Antony did not answer immediately. Each glass was rather overfull and he carried them carefully across the room. When hers was in its usual place Jenny curled up resignedly on the sofa and watched her husband put down his drink on the mantelpiece near the clock and turn to face her. 'He'd probably just quote Johnson at me again,' he said gloomily.

'It's really no use annoying him unnecessarily,' said Jenny sipping her drink.

'That's what I'm saying. Need he ever know?'

'Don't be so silly, Antony. You know what the legal grapevine is like. If Mr Halloran doesn't hear about it and tell Uncle Nick – '

'You're right of course.' He retrieved his drink and took a healthy swig of it. 'I'll go down after dinner,' he decided.

In the event they both went down to the study when the meal was over. The discussion was long and, on Sir Nicholas's part at least, acrimonious. But later – two days later to be exact when Sykes phoned with the information – Maitland was glad he had taken Jenny's advice. There was a quantity of morphine in that one chocolate. 'It might have killed you, might not,' said Sykes laconically. 'Depends on your tolerance for the stuff.' But he too was worried, and subjected Maitland to a short lecture on the subject of taking care which his hearer – still sore from his talk with his uncle – didn't appreciate in the slightest.

For a little while even Jenny's serenity was shaken, she could hardly bear Antony out of her sight; and she went about looking, as her husband described it unflatteringly, very much like a ghost that had just seen its reflection in a mirror. But when a week had gone by and nothing else had happened she began to gain confidence, and long before the trial came on she was looking herself again. The conferences the defence lawyers held didn't seem to be getting anywhere, the only fact to emerge being that Mr Gliddings had moved to Scotland, and certainly hadn't been in London when Douglas Johnstone died . . . negative information at best.

But Jenny, though she would never have admitted it, found this lack of progress a cause of obscure satisfaction.

TUESDAY, 14th DECEMBER

The evening before they were due in court, Sir Nicholas invaded his nephew's room in chambers. An unusual proceeding, particularly on a Tuesday when they would meet later over dinner. It was a long, dark, not particularly comfortable room, especially for the entertainment of visitors, and Sir Nicholas halted in the doorway. 'Good God,' he said, 'how can you work in here?'

'I haven't much choice.' Maitland's amusement was tempered by the realisation that his uncle was in one of his more difficult moods. If that were so, he thought he could make a good guess at the reason. 'You wanted to talk to me about something,' he said tentatively.

'I should have thought that was obvious.' Sir Nicholas's tone was still testy, but suddenly, with one of his abrupt changes, he gave the younger man a companionable grin. 'No holds barred,' he said; and in case Antony might not already have taken the point, added, 'Without the ladies present.'

'That's what I thought,' said Maitland and wandered away to the window.

'You will be in court tomorrow with the Johnstone case – ' ('Well I know that,' muttered Antony rebelliously) ' – and to make matters worse Garfield will be prosecuting.'

'I don't see what that has to do with it.'

'He has a gift for sarcasm; and I have a nasty feeling, Antony, that you are going to invite him to use it.'

Maitland turned and looked squarely at his uncle. 'I've taken chances before,' he said.

'What I think you should realise is that this case is becoming a *cause célèbre*. If you step out of line, there'll be publicity.'

'I'm aware of that,' said Antony, in very much the same tone as he had used before. 'But who said anything about stepping out of line?'

'I know exactly what you are thinking,' said his uncle coldly. 'You have persuaded yourself that both your client and O'Brien's are innocent – '

'Don't you think I have reason? Ever since that stupid affair of the poisoned chocolate.'

'Have you talked to O'Brien about that?'

'Of course I have. I was trying to point out its implications to him, but I can't say I made much impression. His attitude is that there must be any number of people with grievances against me – much the same thing as the police said – and that I'd have to come up with something better than that if I wanted him to take me seriously. Of course, Sykes wasn't quite so blunt; he was making enquiries, he said, which amounted to the same thing.'

'You see!' said Sir Nicholas, as though his point had been proved for him.

'You're telling me that's what you believe is true?'

'I don't know what I believe,' Sir Nicholas admitted. 'But I know you feel strongly about it, something that might have hurt Jenny, and if you lose your temper in court you won't do yourself or your client any good.'

'That's the last thing I'm likely to do.' He moved slowly and rather stiffly across the room and began to rearrange unnecessarily the papers on his desk. Uncle Nick was in the right of it, that was the trouble, and he was painfully aware at that moment of his own limitations.

'Is it?' enquired his uncle sceptically.

There was still time for this conversation to deteriorate into something resembling a brawl. Antony looked up and essayed a smile. 'The trouble is, Uncle Nick, I do believe now they're innocent. I believe too, as you've guessed, that I know who the guilty party is. But as for proving it – '

It was touch and go, but to his relief Sir Nicholas responded quite amiably. 'Just don't let those beliefs of yours prompt you to act unwisely,' he said. And then, inconsequently, 'Vera is going to be in court.'

It was Antony's turn to exhibit surprise. 'Is she though?' He paused, and then added tentatively, 'Are you going with her?'

'I shall be on my feet before Mr Justice Conroy,' and Sir Nicholas. He too hesitated a moment, probably to savour his nephew's evident relief, and then said with a lack of emphasis that made Maitland realise he was very serious indeed, 'I've told you what I think, Antony. Just remember it, that's all.'

PART TWO

REGINA versus
JOHNSTONE and COLLINGWOOD, 1971

WEDNESDAY, the first day of the trial

I

Mr Justice Carruthers was a small man, with a face like an intelligent bloodhound. He had been on the Bench for a long time now, so that there was no denying he was getting on in years, though he looked as spry as ever. There were those among counsel who felt that it was high time he retired, but that was probably because each one felt that the judge's scarlet robes would become him better than the less dramatic black and white. Sir Nicholas, who had once turned down a judgeship on the ostensible grounds that it would be unnerving to encounter his nephew in court in that capacity, was not among them. Nor was Maitland; he liked Carruthers and knew him to be fair, and not so prone to acid comment as some others he could name.

The judge in his turn was not, as so many of his brethren were, at all shocked by Maitland's unorthodox ways; rather, he found them a pleasant source of entertainment. As he looked out across the court that morning the thought was in his mind that with Garfield and Maitland in the same room the sparks were bound to fly. Paul Garfield, now solicitor-general, was a tall man, almost handsome in spite of a prominent, enquiring nose. His morals were puritanical and he was almost as completely without humour as it was possible for a man to be. Those who knew him well would have told you that his strong sense of justice transcended either of these attributes. But Maitland had been right in assuming that the hint of misconduct between the two accused would prejudice him heavily against them.

There was also, the judge thought, the unlikely alliance

133

between Maitland and O'Brien. Or was it an alliance? Each would fight for his own client, that was right and proper, but O'Brien was not known as a patient man, and Maitland on a fact-finding mission could be very annoying indeed. He dismissed their respective juniors without giving them too much attention. It was in the clash of personalities between the three leading counsel that any real interest in the trial would lie.

In its way, as Sir Nicholas had remarked with so much feeling last night, it had become a *cause célèbre*. Mr Justice Carruthers looked over the defendants now, and thought what a pity it was that two nice young people should have taken so horrific a way out of their difficulties. If, indeed, that was what had happened; Maitland had been known to have some surprises for the court before now. Kate was standing stiffly, her face almost expressionless, but as the judge watched she turned and smiled at her fellow-prisoner, and the smile lit up her face to something like real beauty. The man seemed a pleasant enough fellow, though nothing out of the way as far as looks went; but whether he deserved it or not it seemed he had won her affection, and a fine tangle they had made of things between them.

The indictment had been read, chairs had been brought for the prisoners, Paul Garfield rose to make his opening statement. The judge sighed and picked up his pen.

Maitland was aware of O'Brien simmering beside him as he listened, but there was nothing to be done at this point and a series of objections would only alienate the jury. Counsel for the Prosecution might be expected to speak at length, he was a man who apparently hadn't any very great opinion of the collective intelligence of a jury. So every point was hammered home, repeated *ad nauseam*. Maitland heard every damning word, but for all that anyone who didn't know him well could have told he might have been asleep. Fortunately Derek Stringer had thought to warn Richard Kells of this habit of his leader's, so the solicitor remained fairly calm.

And damning was the word for it. Trust Garfield to present his case as effectively as it was possible to do. Antony, opening his eyes for a moment and seeing Kate's pallor and James's strained look, wished, as he had often done before in similar circumstances, that it was possible to explain to them that this was only one side of the story. He would have his turn, O'Brien would have his turn, and O'Brien was a formidable fighter.

But at last it came to an end, the convincing, repetitious account of the state of affairs in the Johnstone household, of Kate's growing friendship with James Collingwood, and of Douglas Johnstone's last day on earth. Maitland opened his eyes and sat up. Garfield was just seating himself again, he had a complacent look; at Antony's side Derek Stringer's hand moved steadily across the paper in front of him, catching up with the note; O'Brien said softly, for Antony's ear only, 'What I tell you three times is true.'

Maitland answered with a rather absent-minded smile. This was part of the evidence he knew by heart, there was nothing for either of them here. Proof of identity; the pathologist, with details of how Douglas Johnstone had died; a man from the laboratory where the hypodermic had been examined for traces of morphine. None of that was under dispute, even Kevin O'Brien wasn't inclined to cavil at the fact that Garfield's junior was blatantly leading his witnesses.

After that the judge adjourned for luncheon. Maitland, glancing up at the gallery and thinking it would be difficult to find Vera in the crush, saw to his surprise that both the Harleys were there. They hadn't entirely abandoned their daughter then, even though she wouldn't take their advice. It's easy enough to be wrong about people, he thought, and perhaps I've been wrong in some of the other conclusions I've reached. But then he saw Vera waving to him, and turned to ask O'Brien to join him and meet his new aunt. Derek

135

Stringer had some affairs of his own to attend to and said, as he so often did, 'I must fly.'

After lunch there was the police evidence, the scene-of-crime people first, and then his old friend or antagonist, whichever you liked to call him, Chief Detective Inspector Conway. At this point Antony made himself unpopular by demanding detailed plans of the house, and got them after some small delay. Conway looked irritated, but then he had never been able to please Conway whatever he did. What was more serious from his point of view was that O'Brien seemed almost equally displeased. 'No use antagonising the chap,' he muttered, 'and what use you think they'll be – '

'You never know,' said Maitland equably. Uncle Nick had warned him against losing his temper, and if he were to do it at this stage of the game, and with his fellow-counsel at that, he thought it would be all up with his client.

And Inspector Conway's evidence, of course, was more or less a repetition of what Counsel for the Prosecution had already told the court. Garfield was treading more carefully now, giving no grounds for an objection. The examination-in-chief seemed to go on forever, but it was over at last, and it was with a tingle of excitement that Maitland watched his learned friend, Kevin O'Brien, get to his feet to cross-examine.

'His Lordship has allowed you to put my client's preliminary statement into evidence, Chief Inspector. Would you say that there is anything in it that particularly points to her guilt?'

That was a novel approach and Conway, quite understandably, looked a little taken aback. 'I should perhaps point out to you,' he said, after a moment's hesitation, 'that there are other witnesses to the fact that Mrs Johnstone did not get on with her husband.'

'We shall come to that in due course. At the moment it is Mrs Johnstone's statement we are considering. She admitted to you freely that she had quarrelled with the deceased?'

'On numerous occasions,' said Conway.

136

'And that she would have left him if it were not for the children,' O'Brien insisted.

'She said so, yes.'

'Don't you think that was a very normal reaction in a woman with strong maternal feelings?'

'I suppose it was.' Conway's tone was grudging. But in his way he was almost as much of a prude as Garfield was, and he couldn't quite leave well alone. 'A more compelling motive would be her liaison – '

'Now that was my next point, Chief Inspector.' O'Brien interrupted quickly, but he did not sound altogether satisfied. 'We have heard a good deal about this so-called liaison, both from you and from my honourable and learned friend, Mr Garfield. I put it to you that "friendship" would be a better word. A lonely young woman with an older, rather serious-minded husband . . . but are we to take this on your word alone, or can you offer us proof?'

Now this question was clearly not to Conway's taste. Maitland watched him and thought, At least I was right about that, Bingham didn't go anywhere near the police. 'Counsel for the Prosecution has mentioned that he will introduce proof,' said Conway, not too sure of himself.

'Proof that a friendship existed. Proof that Dr Collingwood would take tea with Mrs Johnstone after visiting one of the children professionally.' O'Brien's voice poured scorn on anyone who might be unwise enough to draw the wrong conclusion from these not very incriminating facts.

'And that they met almost every afternoon,' said Conway, rallying a little.

'In a teashop? Can you imagine anything more innocent – ?'

The detective was on his mettle now and his sincerity was obvious. 'Since you ask me, sir, I cannot imagine a completely innocent motive for these meetings,' he said.

O'Brien left the subject, and perhaps, thought Antony, that was wise. 'My client will tell us – this is in her statement too, my lord – that her son's illness was sufficient reason for Dr Collingwood to visit the house that afternoon. Would you dispute that, Chief Inspector?'

'In view of Dr Trevelyan's visit in the morning, I think I should.'

'Well, well, Inspector, you're a hard man to please.' These about faces of O'Brien's were confusing to a witness, as Antony knew. 'There is also the matter which my friend says can be confirmed by the parlourmaid's evidence, of a package that is alleged to have passed between the two defendants that afternoon.'

'From Dr Collingwood to Mrs Johnstone. Exactly!' said Conway.

'And which Mrs Johnstone claims contained nothing more sinister than a snapshot of the children, taken by the doctor in the nursery on the occasion of his last visit.'

'That is what she claims,' said Conway stolidly.

'I shall put the picture in evidence in due course.' O'Brien was suspiciously amiable. 'There is just one more matter on which I should like your opinion, and this is an important point, though very simple. Do you really find it so very wonderful, is it really so very incriminating, that a married woman should be seen coming out of her husband's bedroom?' He sat down quickly before the witness could reply, and Maitland came slowly to his feet. It might not seem that his colleague had got very far, but a basis had been laid for his address later on to the jury, and that was all to the good.

'You have some questions yourself for Chief Inspector Conway, Mr Maitland?' enquired Carruthers courteously.

'A few, my lord. I shall not detain the court long. We have heard a good deal of conjecture, a good many inferences have been drawn, from facts that seem to most people to be completely innocent. So if I ask you –'

He got no further. Garfield was on his feet, 'My lord, I protest!' But Maitland was watching Conway, and saw him

138

smile; a smile that said as clearly as words could have done, Just wait till we put our witnesses on the stand. He came in that moment near to throwing caution to the winds, but the remembrance of O'Brien's almost demure cross-examination sustained him.

'I only wanted to ask, my lord,' he said in a tone whose humility Carruthers knew perfectly well to be spurious, 'whether over-anxiety on a doctor's part about an ailing child can be regarded as reprehensible?'

Garfield was still on his feet, but there was no need for his intervention. Carruthers said with some emphasis, 'That is not a question that can properly be put to the Chief Inspector, Mr Maitland.'

'If your Lordship pleases. How soon did you make up your mind about the guilt of the two defendants, Mr Conway?'

It may have been the abruptness of the question that for the moment kept Conway quiet. He glanced from the judge to Garfield and then looked back at Maitland again. 'I have been trying not to jump to conclusions,' he said devastatingly. But spoiled the effect a moment later by adding, 'All the same, the weight of the evidence soon made it apparent to me –'

This time it was Maitland himself who turned an outraged look on the judge. Carruthers coughed, Conway broke off in mid-sentence, and after a moment the judge asked in a kindly tone that ought to have warned his hearers that there might be squalls ahead, 'What exactly are you trying to suggest, Mr Maitland?'

'My lord, it is well known that a preconceived notion is of no help to an investigating officer. I want to know quite simply whether Chief Inspector Conway gave any weight to the other possibilities.'

'What possibilities would those be?' asked Carruthers, interested.

'The possibility that the conspiracy between my client and

139

Mrs Johnstone never existed, my lord. In other words, that someone else killed Douglas Johnstone.'

That caused an outburst of comment among the spectators and the usher bellowed for silence. O'Brien was tugging at Maitland's gown. 'Sit down,' he said, 'and don't make more of a fool of yourself than you can help.'

Antony who had no desire to be at odds with his colleague, gave him a rather vague smile, which did not seem to do much to comfort him. The judge was allowing the silence to lengthen again. His eye had a steely look, and it was with both surprise and relief that Antony heard him say at last, 'I think that is a question that may properly be put, Chief Inspector. But perhaps better by me than by the defence. Did you investigate all possibilities, whether they seemed probable to you or not?'

'I did, my lord.' Conway was stiff with anger now and Maitland thought ruefully that it boded ill for their next meeting. But he had made his point, one to which he might wish to return during the days that followed, and now he could safely leave it. He went on much as O'Brien had done, taking the detective over his statement again, putting matters in the best light he could. It was late afternoon when he had finished and the judge adjourned without further ado.

The prisoners had disappeared from the dock. Kells was asking anxiously, 'How do you think it went?' Antony, looking at O'Brien, saw that the two angry spots of colour in his cheeks that always betrayed him when he lost his temper had faded.

'What did you think?' he asked, passing the question on. And waited with some little trepidation to hear the answer.

'Too early to say.' For the moment all of O'Brien's charm was turned on Richard Kells, and then again for a moment on his own instructing solicitor. When he turned to Maitland it was with a rueful grin. 'Heaven save us from our friends!' he said.

140

II

He managed to find Vera in the crowd, it wasn't often they got such a turnout on the first day of a trial. This one, to his discomfort, as everyone seemed bent on making him realise, seemed to have caught the public imagination, and he wondered how the two defendants felt about that. His own client, he thought, had developed a rather dogged look towards the end of the day, as though he was damned if he was going to let his feelings show; but Kate had begun to wilt visibly. It might be the atmosphere in the courtroom, or it might have been the things she was being forced to hear. However it was, it gave him no pleasure to contemplate; they were going back to one more night behind bars, with the door locked against escape, and now that he had finally made up his mind about their innocence the thought was intolerable.

So he caught up with Vera, and even managed to secure a cab, though this was rather more difficult. Vera, who was never one to talk before she had had time to think, discoursed on a variety of subjects in the taxi, and did not deliver the verdict he was waiting for until he had unlocked the door and followed her into the hall of the house in Kempenfeldt Square.

'Shouldn't have done it, you know,' she said, at her most abrupt.

He didn't pretend to misunderstand her. 'But I wanted to know,' said Maitland reasonably.

That stopped her for a moment while she considered how far it went towards justifying his actions. Finally she shrugged. 'Go your own way, always did,' she said. And then, turning towards the study door which was standing invitingly open, added the invitation, 'Come and have a drink.'

That the door was open, he knew from long experience,

meant that his uncle wanted to see him. It might also mean that Jenny was downstairs keeping Sir Nicholas company, and in this case to his relief, that was how it was. Unless Vera had some dark scheme for getting her husband to reason with him, they might have a reasonably peaceful chat over their sherry. But the trial was on his mind, he couldn't altogether keep away from it. 'I've been meaning to ask you, Vera, what you thought of O'Brien,' he said when the promised refreshment had been supplied.

'A lively mind, thinks on his feet. More sense than I would have thought of an Irishman,' said Vera bluntly.

Antony grinned at that. 'I suppose his Irishness is diluted to some extent,' he said reflectively. 'At any rate, he was born in Yorkshire, Arkenshaw to be exact. Not that he's above assuming a brogue, when it suits him, I suppose he finds it has its effect on some people.'

Sir Nicholas, having greeted his wife and nephew, had relaxed again. 'Was it an interesting day on the whole, my dear?' he asked.

'Garfield is just as you described him to me. Shouldn't be surprised if he thought adultery is synonymous with murder. Of course, today was just the preliminaries. But he's got a strong case, and he's going to exploit every bit of advantage that comes his way.'

Antony, who knew all that already, had his own preoccupations that evening. 'I expect you got a good look at the defendants,' he said.

'What else was I there for?' Vera exchanged a glance with her husband, and in his turn Antony caught Jenny's eye. If those two are going to gang up on me, he thought, life may well become unbearable. But hard on the heels of that another idea, more palatable, emerged. He had said to Jenny once that Vera's arrival in Kempenfeldt Square might probably prove to be the best thing that had happened to the household since she joined it herself, and it might well be that this estimate had been a true one. It occurred to him, not for the first time,

142

that perhaps after all, and in spite of his own and Jenny's presence in the house, Sir Nicholas had not found his bachelor existence altogether satisfactory. There was loneliness for instance . . . He became aware that Vera was still speaking, answering his question about the defendants he supposed.

' – likeable couple,' she was saying. 'And I know you're worried about the children. Doesn't do to get emotionally involved in a case, though.'

And that also was undeniably true. Antony said nothing for a moment, but sat sipping his sherry. After a while he remarked with unaccustomed honesty (that made Sir Nicholas stare, and Jenny start and almost spill her drink), 'If you stop caring about things, you might as well be dead.'

'Now there, my dear boy, you are being unfair,' said Sir Nicholas, and Antony looked up quickly because he knew that that form of address might well spell trouble. 'What Vera meant – '

'I know what she meant. The trouble is, Uncle Nick,' he admitted, 'there are times when it seems to be the only way for me.'

'And this is one of them?' For a moment Maitland thought his uncle was going to launch into a repetition of last night's warning. Instead Sir Nicholas glanced at Vera in what was unquestionably a cautionary way; but for all that, and in spite of his knowledge of his nephew's ways, he himself spoke incautiously. 'You'll do your best,' he said.

That brought Maitland to his feet in a hurry and took him to the window and back. 'That's just the trouble,' he said in a harsh voice. '*I* do my best, and *they* go to prison. Perhaps somebody else, or even O'Brien alone – '

'What does O'Brien think?' asked Sir Nicholas, interrupting this diatribe without scruple.

Perhaps the coolness of his voice had a calming effect; at any rate Maitland laughed, though not with much amusement, and said with a fair assumption of casualness, 'He's not loving me very much at the moment.'

143

'That's a pity. However, I dare say you'll be able to work out your differences. And whatever happens, Antony,' said Sir Nicholas impressively, 'I think you should deal with this case in your own way. You'll regret it if you don't.'

A complete reversal of what had been said last sight. He had been talking to Vera, that was the only explanation. But Vera herself had not approved of the small beginning he had made that day. Sensibly he gave up the problem, sat down again beside Jenny and devoted himself to his sherry.

But good sense was never Maitland's strongest suit, and his bewilderment persisted throughout the evening, even though Jenny, sensing his reluctance, did not again mention the trial. Roger came in, and oddly enough he did not mention the subject either. Antony concluded there must be a conspiracy of silence; which might have annoyed him if he had not, on the whole, been well satisfied with the results.

THURSDAY, the second day of the trial

I

The next day started quietly enough, with the evidence of the waitress from the teashop who had regularly taken Mrs Johnstone's and Dr Collingwood's order. She knew perfectly well who they were, Mrs Johnstone had lived all her life in that neighbourhood, and the young doctor had been the cause of interest and some excitement ever since he had joined Dr Trevelyan as his assistant. For one thing, a doctor should have a wife; for another, Dr Trevelyan was known to be fussy, and it was a matter of speculation whether the newcomer would be able to live up to his ideals.

'Do you remember the last occasion when you saw the two accused together?' Garfield asked her.

She took a moment to assimilate the description. 'It was a Monday, I remember particularly because I was going on my holidays the next week. And I was surprised not to see them all the week, but on Saturday someone came into the teashop and said Mr Johnstone had died. So I thought, if he's been ill, of course his wife would be busy.'

Douglas Johnstone had died on a Friday. After a little skirmishing they got the date settled to Garfield's satisfaction. 'We will return to these . . . meetings . . . between the two accused,' he said. 'Did they seem intimate together?'

'They talked like old friends, if that's what you mean.'

That had not been exactly what Garfield meant, and both Maitland and O'Brien had pricked up their ears at the witness's choice of words. 'Perhaps you would explain to us exactly what you mean by that,' said Garfield, not quite so pleased with her as he had been.

'Well I had to be near the table pretty often, see, serving the tea and like that. Sometimes they stopped talking when I went near the table, and I think perhaps there was something they didn't want me to overhear. But that last day I did hear her say, "I can't stand it any longer, James." And he put out a hand and covered hers, but what he answered her I just don't know.'

'Was that the only occasion – ?'

'The only time I remember.'

Garfield persisted a little longer, succeeded in creating very well an atmosphere of intrigue. When at last he sat down, O'Brien glanced at Maitland who shook his head slightly, giving the other man the green light. O'Brien came to his feet slowly and stood looking at the witness, weighing her up. 'How long have you been working at the Rosebud Teashop?' he asked.

'Well I can't . . . it must be ten years,' she said more positively.

'And in all that time a good many customers must have passed its doors.'

'We're always busy.' His casual tone seemed to reassure her, she was settling down for a good gossip. 'There's lunches, we do light lunches as well as teas, and then we're open until seven o'clock if anybody wants a snack.'

'A good opportunity to study human nature. I expect you've seen and heard a good many strange things in your time.'

'Oh, yes, of course I have. There was the lady with the Pekinese, wanted her to sit on a chair beside her and eat muffins. And a couple who always came in hand in hand, but then read books or magazines the whole time they were there. I could tell you – '

'Yes, I can see you could. You have found the general public an interesting study, and very often odd in its behaviour.'

'I suppose you could say that.' She sounded a little doubtful

146

now, as though perhaps he were leading her past the point to which she wished to go.

'And in view of all these antics you have observed, do you really think that my client's behaviour was so very strange? Or that of Dr Collingwood, for that matter?'

'I never thought anything about it until I heard – '

'Until you heard they had been arrested? No, I'm sure you didn't, madam. There was really nothing strange to think about it.'

Mr Justice Carruthers looked enquiringly at Maitland when O'Brien seated himself again, but Maitland shook his head. 'Thank you, your lordship, my honourable and learned friend has said everything there is to be said on the subject.'

Garfield too having declined to re-examine, the next witness was called.

As soon as he heard the name, Maitland was aware that it was unfamiliar. It didn't need Richard Kell's hand on his shoulder, or his urgent whisper, to confirm the fact. He was about to get up when he saw that O'Brien had forestalled him. Well, let it go, one defence protest would do as well as another.

The witness was a pale young man in a well pressed, rather shabby suit. His name was Cyril Hobart and he was the desk clerk at the Rochester Hotel. Garfield with obvious insincerity apologised to the two defence teams for calling a surprise witness; he had known nothing about Mr Hobart's testimony until that morning. What had happened was that Mr Hobart had seen the accuseds' pictures in the evening paper, realised that what he had to say might be helpful, and very properly gone round to the police station. He (Garfield) regretted any inconvenience there might be to the defence ...

Like hell he does! O'Brien sat down, fuming. This morning it was Maitland's turn to be philosophical. 'At least we knew that this evidence might be forthcoming,' he pointed out. 'Ever since that bloody little man came to see me.'

'You're right, of course.' O'Brien gave him a lopsided grin

147

and subsided. Garfield was already confronting the witness.

'Perhaps you will give the court, Mr Hobart, the gist of the statement you made to the police last night.'

It cannot be said that Cyril Hobart looked altogether comfortable in his new role. A sense of duty, thought Maitland, not without cynicism, can be an uncomfortable thing to have. 'It was seeing that picture in the paper that did it,' said Mr Hobart. 'I thought I recognised them two. Brown, they called themselves when they came to the Rochester.'

There followed some talk about dates, and the hotel register was produced. He remembered the occasion very well, the lady had seemed nervous. They just wanted the room for a few hours so that they could rest after the journey and change before going out in the evening. But he happened to be still talking to the chap who took over from him when they left, and the lady was still wearing the same clothes. And, come to think of it, they hadn't no luggage, neither.

Somehow the scene he conjured up was extraordinarily believable, with Kate in her nervousness talking too much, explaining things that didn't need explaining. Garfield put all the expected questions. Now that he could see the people concerned, was he still absolutely sure of the identification? But he got, to the defence's chagrin, the answers that he obviously expected. The witness might be unhappy at the position in which he found himself, but he was ready to swear on a stack of bibles that Mrs Johnstone and Dr Collingwood were his Mr and Mrs Brown.

It hardly seemed worth while cross-examining, you could only make matters worse. Both Maitland and O'Brien declined the doubtful privilege. Cyril Hobart stood down thankfully, and the next witness was not, to the defence's relief, a surprise at all.

He was a solicitor, named Edward Green, a tall cadaverous man, whom Maitland amused himself by thinking looked more like an undertaker. Kate had consulted him about a divorce – again a diary was produced and the date established,

148

some six months before Douglas Johnstone died – but when they had gone into the details he had had to advise her that nothing could be done. There was a good deal of argument at this point between the various counsel. The judge had already ruled Kate's statement to the police could be produced, and used as a basis for further questioning; O'Brien was of the opinion that certain portions of it should be excluded. In the event the defence carried the day, and Mr Green was allowed to stand down with the best part of his evidence unheard; also, of course, without cross-examination. But when the judge adjourned the hearing until two o'clock, neither O'Brien nor Maitland was in a very happy frame of mind. They had been prepared for some such testimony as Cyril Hobart had given, true, but that didn't make it any the more palatable.

II

Again Vera was in court, and again he looked for her as the crowd began to disperse. He saw her easily enough, she wasn't an easy person to miss, but this time he was startled to see Meg Farrell beside her. Off-hand, he couldn't recall that she had ever been to court before; certainly not when he was appearing, and most likely not at any other time either. So he greeted her with some suspicion. 'I didn't know you were up at this time of the morning, *darling*,' he said disagreeably, mimicking her own too frequent use of the word.

'Nonsense, darling.' Meg was in no degree daunted by his manner. 'I'm always up when Roger leaves for the City. So this morning I thought . . . and Vera said she would be glad of my company.'

Nothing more was said until they were seated in Maitland's favourite restaurant, Astroff's; which was a favourite, for reasons that were obvious, with a great many of the gentlemen of the bar. They could be sure to be left in peace there, unless they were in a hurry, when service would be fast and good. Today, as Mr Justice Carruthers liked to take his own luncheon in a leisurely way, there was no particular hurry.

'Interesting morning,' said Vera, then, 'Good thing you knew beforehand that the police might get hold of that hotel clerk.'

'It was, indeed.' For the moment he ignored Meg, who had ordered her usual Dubonnet and seemed happy enough for once to sit quietly listening to them. 'All the same, I can't say I liked his evidence, and . . . Vera . . . did you see Kate Johnstone's face?'

'Not blind,' said Vera. 'If you're right about that girl, Antony –'

'I am right, about both of them,' said Antony firmly. 'And I wish,' he added, with a glimmer of the humour that was never very far beneath the surface of his thoughts, 'that you could tell me how to set about proving it.'

'I really came,' said Meg, ignoring this question as irrelevant, 'to hear Jean Lamb give her evidence. So it's a good thing you thought to give us lunch, Antony, so that I can come back to court with Vera this afternoon without fainting for lack of nourishment.'

Antony had a frown for that. 'Do you really think it's a good idea?' he asked.

'Why ever not?'

'Well . . . no reason, I suppose.' He thought, but did not add, You say she's a friend of yours, you may not like what I have to say to her, any more than O'Brien will. But he was jerked away from this train of thought by Meg, who added cheerfully,

'Anyway, I saw Ernest in court this morning. And if he can be there, I don't see why I shouldn't be too.'

'Ernest Lamb?' said Antony. For some reason the words came out almost as a shout, and Vera gave him a sharp, interrogatory look.

150

'I don't know the man,' she said; but Meg was answering too.

'Of course he was there, darling, and I think it was sweet of him. He didn't want Jean to feel deserted when she had to go into the witness box.'

'You think . . . look here, Meg, are you sure you want to come back to court? Her evidence will be damaging to the defendants, O'Brien and I have no choice but to question it.'

Meg's smile had, he thought, a little of the feline in it. 'That's why I want to be there,' she said, 'to hear what you make of her between you. Two clever men . . . don't let her make a fool of you, darling.'

For a long moment Antony looked at her. 'You're trying to warn me about something, Meg,' he said at last flatly.

'Well, I thought perhaps you hadn't taken in what I told you the other evening. There's more to Jean than appears on the surface; much, much more.'

'I'm not likely to forget it.' But it was a subject he had no desire just then to discuss at length. He turned instead to Vera. 'What do you think?' he asked. 'The strategy I outlined to you and Uncle Nick – '

'Never knew you ask my advice before,' said Vera gruffly. 'Surely – '

'Should have said. Never known you take it. Not what I'd do myself,' said Vera seriously, 'but if you're sure enough in your own mind you'll go ahead, and nothing I can say will make any difference.'

Antony grinned at that. It was as near as Vera was likely to come to giving him her blessing. He set himself then to amuse his guests with conversation that did not concern the trial, but it couldn't be said that he was sorry when the interlude came to an end.

III

Jean Lamb, the first witness after the recess, was another little woman, with wavy brown hair and hazel eyes. Though she stood very erect she seemed dwarfed by the witness box and looked rather lonely there. Maitland's heart sank when he saw her. There was a softness about her, an impression that she would be everybody's friend, that was bound to go down well with the jury. The greater part of her evidence-in-chief was marred, from the prosecution's point of view, by a spate of objections from O'Brien. Antony couldn't blame him, though he knew – as Kevin himself must have known – that they would prove futile. The other party to the conversations that were being recounted was in court, in the dock, and would be available for cross-examination when the time came for the defence to present their witnesses. So slowly, unwillingly, the facts were extracted; Jean's reluctance was very obvious. She was a friend ('a very close friend,' she added with emphasis) of Kate Johnstone. Of course she had realised over the years, partly from observation, and partly from what Kate had told her, that the marriage was not altogether a happy one. But it was only recently that the accused had admitted that she was in love with another man, and she hadn't said who it was.

'But you were a close friend of hers,' said Garfield insinuatingly. 'I'm sure you must have had some idea –'

That brought the first of O'Brien's objections – more or less a howl of protest – that the judge sustained. Garfield, who Maitland privately thought was holding up rather well under all these interruptions, rephrased his question.

'Have you ever seen your friend, Mrs Johnstone, and Dr Collingwood together?'

'I saw him once at the house, the children had colds.' She hesitated a moment and then added in a rather shy way, 'There was another occasion when Kate and I were having

152

dinner together in a restaurant, when Dr Collingwood and a friend of his came into the same place. But that was sheer accident.'

'Are you so sure of that?'

The witness was obviously distressed by this question. 'I'm not trying to mislead you,' she protested, 'but it's so difficult to be absolutely sure about anything.'

'What was the outcome of this chance encounter?' Garfield, even though this was his own witness, allowed a certain amount of sarcasm to creep into his tone.

'We all had dinner together. It was very pleasant,' she added, as though this might somehow emphasise the innocence of the encounter. 'Of course, Dr Collingwood had attended me once professionally.'

'You're an observant woman, Mrs Lamb,' said Garfield, a piece of sheer flattery, because he certainly knew nothing to prove it. 'What was your impression of the relationship between the two accused?'

That brought Maitland to his feet, a little bewildered that so experienced a man as Garfield should be allowing himself so much latitude. It must be as he himself had said, though only half seriously, that counsel for the prosecution equated proof of adultery with proof of murder. 'My lord!' he said indignantly.

Mr Justice Carruthers was already nodding his head, not waiting for counsel to proceed with his objection. 'Yes, Mr Garfield, I think you must be content with the evidence of fact that you are able to present to us.'

Garfield was far too old a hand to be put out by this sort of thing. His, 'If your Lordship pleases,' came as respectfully as the most captious judge could have wished. He stood a moment longer, surveying the two defence teams with a contemptuous eye, then he turned back to the witness. 'I have no further questions,' he said, and seated himself.

Maitland was tugging his colleague's sleeve. 'This one is mine, O'Brien,' he said urgently.

153

Kevin O'Brien gave him a long look. If the judge had not been showing some signs of impatience, perhaps he would have hesitated longer. 'All right,' he said at last, but Antony was in no doubt of his reluctance.

He came to his feet slowly, bowed to the judge in acknowledgement of the fact that he might well have issued a rebuke about the delay and had not done so, and then gave his attention to the witness. She still had her shy, vulnerable look, and he started his questions in a low key. 'You have told my honourable and learned friend that you are intimately acquainted with Kate Johnstone,' he said, 'and that you have met my client, Doctor James Collingwood, on two or three occasions. I am sure that my friend, Mr O'Brien, will have some questions for you on these matters very shortly, but just now I want to concentrate on something that the prosecution has inexplicably ignored.'

He hadn't meant to stop there, but the witness herself interrupted him, saying, 'So you're Mr Maitland?' in a surprised tone. It was as though the words came of their own volition.

'I am,' said Maitland, and smiled at her. And now he waited.

It seemed necessary to explain herself. 'You see, you came to see Ernest, my husband, so of course I wondered – '

'Of course you did,' he agreed cordially. 'But none of this is relevant to this issue, Mrs Lamb, and my honourable and learned friend is getting impatient.' Another moment, he thought, and Garfield will be on his feet. 'The questions I want to ask you concern the day of Douglas Johnstone's death. You visited the house in Wilgrave Square, did you not?'

'Yes, I did.' Her voice was so low that he could hardly hear her. 'I don't like thinking about that day though.'

'I'm afraid I must ask you to do so.' His tone was still gently courteous, but she raised her eyes then to meet his, and he was startled at the fierceness of her look. 'In fact, I

154

must ask you to tell me in some detail exactly what happened on that visit. To begin with, at what time did you arrive?'

'It was . . . oh, I suppose it was about half past four.'

'Who let you in?'

'Why, Sophie of course.'

'My lord!' Garfield had come to his feet without haste, and his voice as he went on reflected – or purported to reflect – a certain boredom. 'This matter is irrelevant,' he pointed out.

'What have you to say to that, Mr Maitland?'

'My honourable and learned friend, my lord, has had his fun with this witness.' That was deliberate provocation, the use of the word 'fun' in connection with one of Garfield's intensely serious examinations was so inappropriate as to be ludicrous. 'There are still a few facts I wish to elicit. Is that too much to ask?'

'In the circumstances, Mr Garfield,' said Carruthers, with all his customary courtesy, 'I think I must disallow your objection. However, Mr Maitland – '

Antony was in no doubt as to how to take that. He was being warned to walk warily, and that was just what he intended to do. 'So Sophie let you in,' he said. 'Did you have any talk with her?'

'I said good afternoon, of course. I know her quite well.' The witness had still some surface self-possession, but he thought he could discern the beginnings of nervousness. 'Then she said that Kate was in the drawing-room, and I went straight in there because we never stood on ceremony. And, of course, I knew my way.'

'And was Mrs Johnstone in the drawing-room?'

'I've just told you – '

'You have told me what Sophie said, Mrs Lamb. She might have been mistaken.'

'Well, she wasn't! Kate was there – '

'Alone?'

'Yes, she was.'

155

'What was she doing? Reading? Sewing?' He could sense Garfield's uneasiness now at a line of questioning he couldn't understand, and that couldn't be expected to do the defence any good. But more than that he was aware of O'Brien beside him, of a sort of smouldering anger that was not characteristic . . . with Kevin's temper it was usually quick come, quick go. 'What was Mrs Johnstone doing?' He repeated, when Jean Lamb seemed in no hurry to answer his question.

'She was . . . just sitting.'

'Did you make any comment on that?' He was trying for a light tone. 'A penny for your thoughts . . . something like that?'

'I did, I asked her . . . because it wasn't like Kate to be idle.'

'And she told you what she was thinking about?' Garfield made a move as though to get up, but decided against it. After all, when he had had his turn with the witness, O'Brien's objections had got short shrift. A moment later he was glad enough that he had held his tongue.

'She told me she had just done something dreadful,' said Jean Lamb clearly. That brought a gasp from the spectators. Maitland wasn't at all sure that his own colleagues hadn't joined in. But this was no time to allow himself to be distracted from what he was doing. 'I'm sure you didn't leave it there, Mrs Lamb,' he said. 'You asked her what she meant, and she told you.'

'Yes, of course.'

'And now you are going to tell us.' That was said in an encouraging tone, but again he got one of those looks of hers. He thought she hesitated a moment, perhaps hoping for Garfield's intervention, but when she saw that there was no help for it she answered clearly enough.

'She said James had been there earlier in the afternoon, and she'd sent him away for good.'

'Now that's very interesting, in view of what is alleged to

156

have passed between them that day. You didn't think to mention this to my friend for the prosecution?'

'He didn't ask me,' said Jean Lamb simply. Something in her tone caused a ripple of amusement among the spectators. 'And I can't see that it is so very important anyway,' added the witness defiantly.

'Can't you?' He allowed his scepticism to be apparent. 'Well, I must take your word for that, Mrs Lamb. What was said next?'

'Nothing.'

'Come now,' – encouragingly – 'how long were you with her?'

'About an hour, I suppose.'

'Then I'm sure you didn't sit in silence all that time.'

'Of course not.' She seemed fond of the words 'of course'; perhaps to her they symbolised the contempt she felt for his questions. 'I sympathised with her, you know, but I could quite see that it was the right thing to have done.'

'That means – doesn't it? – that you believed what she told you.'

For the first time Jean Lamb looked straight at the woman in the dock. 'She is my friend,' she said ambiguously. But then added, before Maitland could do anything to stop her, 'If you must have the truth, I don't think she would have been able to keep that resolution.'

'I see.' He thought he did, but he could quite sympathise with what O'Brien must be feeling. The help he had wanted would have been given outside the courtroom, not in what must seem quite futile cross-examination of the prosecution's witnesses; probably by now he was under the impression that he had unwittingly conjured up the devil. 'Was my client, Dr Collingwood, the sole topic of conversation that afternoon?' asked Maitland, as smoothly as if he had never been distracted by a thought that at any other time he would have found amusing.

'No, he wasn't. Kate didn't seem to want to talk about

157

that at all. I tried to get her mind off it by asking about the children, Dougie hadn't been well, you know.'

If Maitland had been intent before, as he always was when dealing with a witness, there seemed to be something added to his concentration now. 'Had Mrs Johnstone anything else to say about that?'

'Only that he was better, really, so that it seemed silly that both the doctors had been in that day. But he was still a little listless, and Janet – '

'What about Janet?' asked Maitland sharply. He hadn't meant to speak in quite that tone, and he needn't have interrupted the witness, who was obviously about to tell them.

'She was bored, having no-one to play with. And that's really all.'

'The rest of your conversation – ?'

'Kate wasn't a very lively companion that day. I don't really remember what we talked about, I expect I was trying to find something to take her mind off things. But I didn't stay very long, because I wanted to get home before Ernest – before my husband did.'

'But before you left the house you went upstairs?'

'Yes, of course. Sophie would have given my things to Daisy to put in Kate's room. She always did that.'

'You know the layout of the bedroom floor pretty well then?'

That was too much for Garfield. He came to his feet with an indignant swirl of his gown. 'My lord!' he said. 'This line of questioning has gone far enough.'

'Too far perhaps.' Mr Justice Carruthers's tone had a suspicious amiability. 'Mr Maitland, I appreciate the importance of the events of that day, but if there was no further conversation between the witness and Mrs Johnstone – '

'There wasn't, my lord,' said Jean quickly.

' – then I think you have elicited all the facts that can be deemed relevant.'

'That, my lord – '

'No, Mr Maitland,' said the judge, with finality.

'If your lordship pleases.' Counsel had a mutinous look, but there was nothing for it but to sit down again, and in doing so encounter a furious look from O'Brien. Kevin had the flush high on his cheekbones that Antony had first noticed when they were opponents in a case in the North of England, and that he had since learned meant trouble. He didn't let this worry him overmuch, however, it was only what he'd expected.

O'Brien's cross-examination did not delay the court for long, and was confined exclusively to the points brought out by Garfield in direct examination. There was not much to be done in that direction, as Maitland had felt instinctively; but, of course, if O'Brien could succeed in making things sound better for his client it was his job to do so. In any event, he was watching his step, nothing of moment emerged, and it wasn't long before he was sitting down again, this time without a glance in his colleague's direction.

The next witness was the Douglas Johnstones' house-keeper, a dragon of a lady, completely in sympathy with Garfield's aims. Too much in sympathy perhaps for the prose-cution's interests, counsel spent half his time trying to tone down her obvious dislike of her mistress. She had known something was going on, they all had, and there had been words passed between Mr and Mrs Johnstone on more than one occasion. O'Brien contented himself with emphasising what Garfield had sought to minimise, there wasn't really much else to be done; and when Maitland's turn came he declined to cross-examine.

The next witness, the nursemaid, Helen Gatsby, was on the other hand only too obviously in sympathy with Kate. Paradoxically, this probably did the defence more harm than good, and it lent credence to the evidence that Garfield ex-tracted from her with a good deal of difficulty. To the best of her recollection she had always been present when Dr Collingwood had visited the children, and Mrs Johnstone,

159

who was a very loving mother, was generally there as well. At first, of course, the visits had been strictly professional, but as time went on she couldn't help but notice that they were . . . fond of one another. She didn't mean anything wrong by that, they had always behaved perfectly correctly. 'But in the presence of the children, that was only to be expected,' suggested Garfield smoothly.

This time it was O'Brien who declined to cross-examine. Maitland got up slowly, seeking in his mind for the right approach. 'I believe I understood you to say, Miss Gatsby, that there was always a good reason for Dr Collingwood's visits.'

She answered that quite eagerly. 'Oh, yes, there was. One or other of the children . . . Dougie isn't always very well, you know.'

'So I have heard. I'm grateful for your confirmation on that point, Miss Gatsby,' he went on. 'Dr Collingwood came when it was professionally necessary to do so, and Mrs Johnstone did no more than any affectionate mother would in being present while he examined the children.'

'That's quite true.'

'So we come to the day of Douglas Johnstone's death. I expect you remember it very well.'

'It isn't the kind of thing one likes to think about, but of course I do.'

'You remember that both the doctors came to see the children? Were you surprised to see Dr Collingwood in the afternoon, after Dr Trevelyan's visit that morning?'

'I think – ' She sounded hesitant, but then went on more firmly, 'I think it was really Dr Trevelyan I was surprised to see.'

Well, that was one risky question that had had a good result. 'Why was that?' he asked.

'Because he hadn't been visiting the children lately. It was always Dr James . . . our doctor, the children used to call him.'

160

No telling how that would go down with the jury. 'Were you with the children all day?'

'Except that they went downstairs for lunch with their mother and Uncle Charles,' she told him. And went on without prompting, 'Dr Collingwood came up alone that afternoon. Mrs Johnstone didn't come with him.'

'What else do you remember about that day?'

'That Dougie was restless. Better, but not *quite* better, you see. And Janet wanted him to play with her, but he was too tired, I think. That made her restless too, she has so much energy.'

'Not an easy day for you, having to keep an eye on them both.'

'She was in and out of the nursery like a Jack-in-the-box,' said Miss Gatsby reminiscently. And without any further questions, to the obvious surprise of the court, Maitland gave her unexpectedly a brilliant smile, thanked her, and sat down.

IV

The judge adjourned after that, until the following morning. Maitland was gathering together his books and papers. 'I shan't be going back to chambers,' he told Willett, handing them over. And then, turning so that he could look from Richard Kells to Geoffrey Horton, 'I'd like to see our clients again, if you can arrange it.'

Richard said, 'Now?' But Geoffrey, more used to his friend's ways, said only, 'No difficulty about that,' and took his fellow solicitor's arm.

O'Brien had been speaking to his junior, but turned now and said to Maitland in the same furious tone he had used before, 'There are a few things we should discuss first.'

Maitland turned to face him, and unwisely let a gleam of

amusement show. 'Regretting the impulse that brought you to Kempenfeldt Square that night?' he asked.

'I want to know what the hell you think you're getting at. What good did it do, that exhibition this afternoon?'

'If you're referring to my cross-examination of Jean Lamb –'

'I am!'

' – Carruthers didn't let me go as far as I'd hoped, but I satisfied myself of her malice.'

'That gentle creature!' said O'Brien explosively.

'If you didn't hear it for yourself I doubt if I can explain it to you.' Maitland sounded suddenly weary. 'All her comments were two-edged, even when she seemed to be defending her I'm sure she did Kate more harm than good.'

'But why Mrs Lamb? God knows, Maitland, I've known you had something in mind, but I didn't know it would lead you to make fools of us both like this.'

'You might remember,' – Antony's voice was as quiet as his uncle's might have been – 'that I too have some cause for anger.'

'If you mean that blasted box of chocolates, there's nothing to say that was anything to do with this case at all.'

'You'll forgive me if I disagree with you. It was all too pat. I asked my questions, one weekend last month. And on the Monday evening the chocolates arrived.'

O'Brien's anger seemed to be cooling somewhat, and when he spoke again he sounded more bewildered than anything else. 'But the police made enquiries, the shop couldn't remember who had bought that particular box. And there weren't any fingerprints on the wrapping, or anything about the card to give any clue at all. So I ask you again, Maitland, why Mrs Lamb?'

'Somebody didn't like my asking questions.'

'I'll grant you that if you like,' said O'Brien, weakening, 'but it still doesn't explain –'

'Someone who knew this much about us,' said Maitland, 'that Jenny doesn't eat chocolates at all, and that I only like almond-flavoured ones. And I dare say you think,' he added with a certain savagery, 'that I ought to be grateful that so much care was taken not to injure her. But I'm not capable of quite so much forbearance, I'm afraid.'

'You still haven't told me –'

'No, I haven't, have I? Of the people I questioned there are three points that made me concentrate on the Lambs. Ernest had a motive; Jean was actually in the house that day; and they're the only ones who might have known our tastes in sweetmeats.'

'How on earth could that have come about?'

'Through the Farrells, of whom you have heard me speak. They're acquainted with the Lambs. Meg doesn't like gossip, but if – if I happened to be in the news at a time when the two families were meeting, the talk might have turned our way, and some of our foibles might have been mentioned.'

'Have you asked Mrs Farrell?'

'She does remember that Jenny and I were mentioned once. It was just after . . . well, that doesn't matter, but there had been some danger. I'm pretty sure she'd have changed the subject as soon as she could, but you can see it might well have led to some such exchange of information as I'm postulating.'

'I can see that, but –'

'Roger doesn't remember anything at all; well, I don't suppose he was listening. All the same, O'Brien, it's the only possible connection, and if you want to save our clients it's the only starting point we have.'

The court was clearing now, but Garfield, still talking to his junior, looked round in surprise as Kevin O'Brien's voice rose to an outraged squeak. 'But Kate Johnstone herself gives Jean Lamb an alibi,' he pointed out.

'An alibi I'd like to break.'

163

'Yes, I can see now what you're after. If Carruthers hadn't stopped you . . . all the same, do you think Kate would have deliberately lied about a thing so much in her favour?'

'Not deliberately, no. I think the whole visit was so ordinary in her mind that she just never gave it much consideration at all. And we know how unwilling she is to suspect her friends.'

'I still think . . . look here, have you any more questions of the same kind to ask the prosecution witnesses?'

Maitland looked at him. He was tired, and his shoulder was aching, and there was a job to be done that he didn't see his way to finishing satisfactorily. All the same, a wave of liking, almost of affection, for the other man came over him and he smiled. O'Brien might be a great one for tilting at windmills, but he had his own methods and they weren't Maitland's. Now he was definitely outraged, so, 'Who are the prosecution calling in the morning?' Antony asked.

'Sophie, the parlour maid, and Dr Trevelyan.'

'I'm afraid I have some awkward questions for them too.'

'But you can't . . . even if you're right there's no way of proving that Jean was ever out of Kate's company.'

'There may be a way, one more witness I must see. Well, I've seen her before, but this evening – ' He let the sentence trail there, and smiled again. O'Brien, he thought, had suffered enough for one day.

The interview with the two defendants was short and, to Antony, painful. Kate seemed to have sunk into apathy; he thought privately that it was the nursemaid's evidence that had upset her, with its mention of the children whom she missed so much. As for Jean's visit, she seemed to have closed her mind completely to the events that preceded her husband's death. They got nothing out of her, she didn't even seem to be interested in why the questions were being asked.

James Collingwood, however, was as full of questions as O'Brien had been, and none of them answerable at this stage. Maitland heaved a sigh of relief when at last they left their

164

clients in the interview room below the court, but O'Brien was still thoughtful and left him in the street outside with the curtest of farewells.

V

He went straight from the Old Bailey to the Charles Johnstones' house, where his welcome – he had this at least to be thankful for – was kindly. There was a little surprise for his request, but it was readily agreed to. The children were having their high tea but as soon as they had finished Janet would be fetched. Meanwhile, surely a drink would not come amiss.

So he waited with what patience he could muster, and presently Felicity went away and returned ushering Janet before her. Luckily she seemed to remember him quite well and came to stand confidingly by his knee as she had done on his previous visit.

'Mummy still hasn't been to see us,' she told him.

He could lie when the occasion warranted it, though to do so always made him uneasy. But to lie to a child was quite beyond him. 'It's difficult for her just now,' he said lamely, 'but she's quite well, you know, and thinking of you.'

Janet regarded him gravely for a moment, to his discomfort, but fortunately the answer seemed to satisfy her. 'I'd like to see our doctor too,' she said. Obviously she had not forgotten their previous conversation.

'I hope that doesn't mean you're feeling ill,' he asked in a teasing tone.

'No, we're quite well. Even Dougie –'

'The last time you saw Dr Collingwood – ' he said, hopefully.

'The day before we came to live here,' Janet nodded. He wondered by what means her childish mind worked out that euphemism for the day her father died.

165

'There's something else I want to ask you about that day,' he told her, 'Do you mind?'

'N-no.' She sounded doubtful, which worried him, but his conscience was eased a moment later when she added, 'Not if I remember.'

'This is about the afternoon, after Dr Collingwood had left. You stayed in that day because Dougie wasn't well enough to go out yet. And I think – I've been told – that he wasn't feeling well enough to play with you.'

'Poor Dougie,' Janet sighed.

'So you had to find a way of amusing yourself.'

'It was so dull in the nursery.'

'So you came out on to the landing, perhaps. Not just when Dr Collingwood left, but later on.'

'Yes, I did. I could run up and down there, and slide.'

'What did Miss Gatsby think of that?'

'Nanny? Oh, she got very cross with me after a while. So when she heard me calling to Mummy she came out and asked her to come up and speak to me.'

'What was your mother doing when you called to her?'

'She went into her bedroom with Auntie Jean. And then when she heard me she came out again, and Miss Gatsby came out of the nursery and asked her to come up.'

'Can you tell the time?'

It obviously seemed to Janet the most unreasonable question yet. 'Of course I can. I'm nearly seven,' she said, quite crossly.

'Then do you remember what time it was when Mummy came upstairs?'

That caused a moment's thought. 'Well, not because I looked at the clock,' she said after a moment. 'But Mummy did because she said, "Their tea will be up in ten minutes and that should give her something to occupy her".'

'And what did you deduce from that? I mean, what time do you have your tea?'

166

'Always at half past five. So you see, it was twenty past five when Mummy came upstairs,' added Janet triumphantly.

'How long was she with you?'

'Well . . . she looked at Dougie's jigsaw puzzle for one thing. I don't think he'd got very far with it. So she did some of the sky for him, that's the difficult part. And she talked for a while to me; you know, Mummy is never really cross, but she did tell me I ought to be more considerate of Dougie.' There was an attempt at mimicry there, and he smiled at her.

'Five minutes, perhaps?' he suggested.

'Yes, perhaps.' She took hold of his sleeve suddenly and tugged at it as if she had not already got all his rather strained attention. 'When you see Mummy, tell her I'm being considerate now,' she said.

He stayed with the Johnstones for half an hour after she had left them, it seemed the least he could do. But as he made his way home he was thoughtful; he was taking himself to task for a missed opportunity that afternoon.

VI

Luckily they were left in peace until after dinner, when Sir Nicholas and Vera arrived together, demanding a blow-by-blow account of the day's action in court. 'But you were there, Vera,' said Antony, bewildered.

'Couldn't make head nor tail of what you were doing,' said Vera frankly.

'Besides,' said Sir Nicholas, at his most languid, 'Halloran called me on the telephone. He said you were up to your old tricks.'

'Now that I call unjust.' Maitland was indignant. 'If I'm not to be allowed to put on a proper defence for my client – ' He broke off there and then added gloomily, 'Anyway, Carruthers wouldn't let me go as far as I wanted.'

'Which was probably just as well.'

'But if the woman is guilty . . . damn it all, Uncle Nick, you wouldn't want me to let her get away with it.'

'You have explained all that to me, I may say exhaustively,' said Sir Nicholas. 'Proving that somebody else *could* have committed the murder is not necessarily going to get you a Not Guilty verdict.' A truth that Antony did not particularly wish to hear propounded just then.

Maitland didn't reply immediately. Instead he left the fireside to pour brandy for their guests, and only when he was back in place on the hearthrug again did he say, carefully casual, 'You haven't heard what I've been doing since I left the court.'

'Wondered where you'd got to,' said Vera.

'Which reminds me.' Antony turned a little to address her more directly, 'What did Meg make of the afternoon's proceedings?'

'Said she thought you were clever, the way you handled the witnesses,' Vera told him.

'That's all she knows about it. As a matter of fact, I made a pretty good hash of things,' Antony confessed. Vera looked sympathetic, but his uncle levered himself a little more upright in his chair.

'That is a particularly unfortunate phrase. I do wish,' Sir Nicholas complained, 'that you could find some way of expressing yourself without resorting to colloquialisms.'

'I wasn't thinking,' said Antony hastily.

Sir Nicholas was following his own train of thought. 'If it wasn't such an important case – ' he said, and then corrected himself quickly. 'Well every case is important, I suppose, to the defendant at least. But the publicity attached to this one makes it particularly unfortunate that you have chosen to meddle.'

'Haven't told us where you went after we adjourned,' said Vera. She wasn't sure whether the answer would provoke another protest from her husband, but Antony was obviously determined to give it.

'To see Janet Johnstone,' he said, and did not for the moment attempt to amplify that simple statement.

Jenny, who had so far been sitting quietly sipping her after-dinner drink, said anxiously, 'You haven't told me that either, Antony. For some reason it worries you, doesn't it?'

'She's six years old. Nearly seven,' he added, with a reminiscent smile for Janet's boasting. 'And she – she's a trusting little thing.' That was the trouble of course, people trusted you and you let them down. And Uncle Nick was in the right of it, there wasn't any proof.

Sir Nicholas settled back in his chair again. 'Why did you go to see her?' he asked idly, which didn't deceive any of his hearers for a moment.

Suddenly Antony smiled. 'You're not going to like this Uncle Nick,' he prophesied. 'It was the damnedest bit of luck, she told me exactly what I wanted to hear, but it was pure guesswork that led me to her.'

'Are we to hear what she told you?' That was his uncle's gentlest tone, it was beginning to be obvious that he didn't like what he had heard of the day's events. Antony was pretty sure that Vera wouldn't have stirred anything up, but Bruce Halloran was one of Sir Nicholas's closest friends, and he wouldn't have pulled his punches. It was one of the mysteries of life how he always managed to be the first to hear any gossip that might be going the rounds.

'Of course I'm going to tell you,' said Maitland, and proceeded to do so, briefly. When he had finished, his uncle nodded approvingly.

'A fact!' he said. 'The first one you've elicited in this business, so far as I recall. If you can trust a child of that age.'

'I think I can.'

'The question remains, what are you going to do with it?'

'Recall the nursemaid. That's the mistake I mentioned, I ought to have got all this out of her.'

'And then?'

'I'll call the child, if I have to.'

169

'You have done that before and got away with it,' said Sir Nicholas consideringly, 'but –'

'If you mean Clare Canning, you called her yourself.' That was Jenny, interrupting indignantly. Sir Nicholas gave her a cold look.

'At your husband's instigation, my dear,' he said. And then, relenting, 'But I admit, it was the right thing to do.'

'Don't like to remind you –' Vera began.

'I know, I know, evidence of opportunity is not proof of guilt.'

'Not what I was going to say. There's still the morphine to explain away.'

'And Dr Trevelyan will be giving evidence tomorrow.'

'Is that relevant?' wondered Sir Nicholas.

'The morphine must have come from his surgery, Uncle Nick. There may be something –'

'Something that he didn't tell the police?' Sir Nicholas didn't think much of that suggestion.

'You know as well as I do, it's often a question of being asked the right things.'

'And that is what you are going to do tomorrow?' enquired his uncle satirically. His glass was empty, and when Antony had refilled it he allowed the subject to drop, and went on to talk about less controversial things.

Maitland was relieved at being granted this temporary truce, but he didn't sleep well that night.

FRIDAY, the third day of the trial

I

When he came into court the next morning, Mr Justice
Carruthers, a man sensitive to atmosphere, was immediately
aware of a coolness between the two leading defence counsel
that had not been there before. If it had not seemed so unlikely, he would almost have said that Kevin O'Brien looked
nervous. The situation was not without its humour, for he
was well aware that Kevin had interested Maitland in the
matter in the first place; now he was reaping where he had
sowed, and in view of Maitland's reputation he should have
been prepared for fireworks. There were certain similarities
between the two men, despite their obvious differences of
temperament: each had a conscience, each was sometimes
over-scrupulous. Where the difference lay was in the way they
dealt with these emotions. O'Brien, a passionate campaigner
for what he believed to be right, would still not take the
further step necessary to lay the blame elsewhere than on his
client's shoulders. Maitland, much less sure of himself, was
all the same prepared to go the whole way, a fact which
O'Brien should have taken into consideration before he made
his appeal.

So the judge watched them, and hid his amusement;
noticing at the same time that the tension between the two
leaders had spread itself to their respective entourages. Garfield was looking disapproving, nothing very unusual there,
but the disapproval deepened when Maitland came to his
feet without waiting for the first witness to be called. 'I
should like permission, my lord, to have one of the prosecution's witnesses recalled,' he said, when at last he succeeded
in catching Carruthers's eye.

171

'Which of the witnesses is that, Mr Maitland?'

'Miss Helen Gatsby, the Johnstone children's nursemaid. With Your Lordship's permission, of course, and that of my honourable and learned friend, Mr Garfield.'

'May I ask the reason for this request?'

'A matter has come to my notice, my lord – ' He did not attempt to elaborate on that, but stood waiting while the judge pondered.

'Do you concur in this request, Mr O'Brien?' Carruthers asked at last.

As clearly as if Maitland had spoken, O'Brien was aware of the stress he was under. And all of a sudden his own indignation over what he felt was an indiscretion – no, a series of indiscretions – left him. 'I have no questions for the witness myself, my lord,' he replied, 'but I do agree with Mr Maitland that the matter he has mentioned should be clarified.'

'Very well.' The judge inclined his head. 'Mr Garfield, I feel that in the circumstances we should agree to Mr Maitland's request.'

'If your lordship pleases.' Given the judge's opinion, there was really nothing left for Garfield to say. Not that he seemed to acquiesce with any great pleasure, but that was the least of Antony's worries at the moment.

He gave O'Brien a grateful smile as he sat down again and muttered: 'Thanks for backing me up.'

There was a short pause while Miss Helen Gatsby was produced, returned to the witness stand, and reminded that she was still on oath. When the judge glanced at Counsel for the Prosecution, Garfield only shook his head. 'Very well then, Mr Maitland,' said Carruthers invitingly.

'A small matter, Miss Gatsby,' said Maitland. He thought she looked nervous, which was only natural in the circumstances, she must wonder what was in the wind. 'The day of Douglas Johnstone's death, you were with the children in the nursery in the afternoon?'

'Yes, I was, but –'

'Can you elaborate on that a little?'

'I don't know what you want me to say. Dr Collingwood came – '

'Yes, so you told us. It is later in the afternoon I am concerned with now. Think about it for a moment.'

The witness paused obligingly, but still did not seem sure what was expected of her. 'It was such an ordinary day,' she said at last. 'Dougie hadn't been well, you know; he was doing a jigsaw, but I don't think he was very interested in it.'

'And Janet?'

'It was nearly time for them to go back to school, and I must say I wished they had started already,' said Miss Gatsby fervently. 'I tried to get her interested in a book, but I think she spent more time on the landing than she did in the room with us.'

'Ten minutes before teatime,' said Maitland. It was obvious that he was quoting, and Garfield looked at him sharply. 'Does that remind you of anything?'

'Oh, yes, of course. Mrs Johnstone came up. I heard Janet calling to her, so I thought I'd ask her to speak to the child. It might quiet her down a little.'

'Do you know what Mrs Johnstone was doing when you called to her?'

'Yes, because she said she couldn't stay more than a minute, Mrs Lamb was in her bedroom putting on her outdoor things.'

'Only a minute?' asked Maitland quietly. And that was a risk, if ever he had taken one.

'That's what she said.' Miss Gatsby smiled. 'But she never could resist the children, you know; she spent a little time helping Dougie with his puzzle, and then of course she had to give as much time to Janet, besides telling her to be a good girl, which she wasn't very that day.'

'How long would you say then, that Mrs Johnstone spent in the nursery?'

'Five minutes at the very least, but I believe it was nearer ten.'

'While Mrs Lamb was alone on the floor below . . . the floor where the bedrooms are?' said Maitland, and sat down quickly before Garfield could protest. 'Painless extractions a speciality,' he said, with a rather lopsided grin at his learned friend, Mr O'Brien.

Garfield had his say. As Maitland remembered from previous encounters, he had a nice turn of sarcasm when he wished, and this morning the judge was giving him full rein. There was also a good deal of noise going on among the spectators. 'That's put the cat among the pigeons,' said O'Brien, but he seemed to have reconciled himself to Antony's tactics, a state of mind which he explained himself a moment later. 'After all,' he said thoughtfully, 'if one conjures up the devil – !' And couldn't understand why Maitland's smile deepened at this echo of his own thought.

But things quietened down again presently, even Garfield's indignation spent itself, and the next witness could be called. This was the parlourmaid, Sophie, to whom Maitland took an immediate dislike. She had another name, of course, but he had never bothered to memorise it. Now he looked at her and thought immediately, a mean-natured woman. And then thought ruefully what Jenny would have said to him for making such a rash judgement.

Garfield was at his best here, being perfectly well aware that he had been right in calling so important a witness late in the game. There was nothing elicited that was new to the defence team, but both Maitland and O'Brien were conscious of each point as it was made, and of how well it went down with the jury. Her evidence started quietly enough, with details of quarrels she had overheard between Kate and her husband. 'Not that I could help hearing,' she added with a sniff. 'Didn't think I was human, I suppose, might as well have been a piece of furniture for all the notice they took.' Garfield lingered over the details until there could be no

174

doubt at all that the jury had taken them in. Then he went
on to the still more damaging point of James Collingwood's
visit to the Johnstone house on the fatal afternoon.

'Mrs Johnstone met him in the hall,' Sophie said. 'She
ordered tea, well I was expecting that. And he was only a
minute or two upstairs, not worth coming for at all if you
ask me. So then they were together in the drawing-room.'

'You took the tea to them there?'

'Yes, I did.'

'Is there anything you wish to tell us about that occasion?'

'They were standing close together on the hearthrug. I
saw him pass her something; no, I couldn't see what it was,
a package wrapped in tissue paper.'

There was some argument there about the size of the
package, but she was vague about it, couldn't remember any
details. Garfield left the question at last. 'Did any words pass
between the two accused while you were in the room?' he
asked.

'She thanked him for what he had given her.' Her tone was
reserved. Maitland had the thought that there might be something here, and the same thing had evidently occurred to
O'Brien for he made a note on his pad. 'How long did Dr
Collingwood stay?' Garfield was asking.

'Not long really, about half an hour I'd say.'

'Were you asked to see him out?'

'No, but I heard him go, so I came into the hall and she
was just going upstairs.'

'Mrs Johnstone?'

'Who else?'

'What did you do then?'

'I cleared away the tea things, of course. They hadn't
eaten anything. And then I thought I'd like to freshen up,
being it was the time of day there might be callers. So I went
up the back stairs to the bathroom on the first floor.'

'Not to your own room?'

'All those stairs? Not on your life.'

'But you saw Mrs Johnstone again a few moments later?'
(Leading the witness, but not worth making a protest. None
of this was under dispute.)

'Yes I did, I saw her coming out of her husband's room.
And I thought, that's a change, that is. Must be months since
she was in there.'

This time O'Brien's protest was vehement, but the ensuing
argument with Garfield did nothing, Maitland thought, to
advance the defendant's case. Sophie's spite was evident, but
the jury had no reason to doubt that she was telling the truth,
and by the time the judge had given his ruling the point would
be firmly fixed in their collective mind. The female prisoner
went her own way, did not share her husband's room, but
had been unaccountably seen coming out of it on the afternoon before he died.

After that there was the usual repetition, with Garfield
making perfectly sure that his points were well hammered
home. He was probably right about that; a careful man, a
precise man, who usually succeeded in his undertakings.
When at last he thanked his witness and sat down, it was
O'Brien who rose to cross-examine, but he hadn't many
questions to ask.

'You were in Mr Johnstone's employment before he
married, weren't you?' he began.

'Three years before. That's thirteen years I'd been with him
when he died.'

'How long had he been paying you to spy on his wife?'

'Why, I – ' She had not expected that, and glanced rather
wildly at the judge as if she thought he might protect her.
When he only looked back at her gravely she turned again to
O'Brien and said sulkily, 'It wasn't like that really. It was
only natural he wanted to know what was going on.'

'And what did you tell him?'

'They was in love, them two, the ones you're defending.'
An incautious question, but probably in the long run the

176

answer made little difference. Maitland watched O'Brien wriggle his shoulders under his gown, as though ridding himself of an unpleasant thought.

'You didn't tell me how long Mr Johnstone had been paying you,' he said.

'About nine months, more or less.'

'You don't like Mrs Johnstone, do you?'

'Why should I? Nothing but trouble there hasn't been since she came to the house.'

'You mean, it made more work for you?'

'Of course it did, with the children and all.'

'Then let us go back to the brief visit Dr Collingwood paid to the house on the afternoon of the murder. A package was handed over, which you don't seem to be able to describe very well. Could it have contained photographs?'

'Is that what she says?' O'Brien didn't answer that, just stood waiting. 'Well, I suppose it could,' said the witness at last, grudgingly.

'You say she thanked him, and that is the only conversation you heard. Are you quite sure Dr Collingwood said nothing at all?' But he added quickly, before she could speak, 'Perhaps this would be a good opportunity to remind you, madam, that you are under oath.'

She took her time to think that out. 'Well, he did say something,' she conceded at last.

'I'm afraid you are going to have to tell us what it was.'

Clearly she didn't want to, but at some time she must have heard that perjury could be a perilous business. 'He said, In that case, Kate, this is the only memento I can give you.'

'How did he sound when he said that?'

Garfield half came to his feet, but subsided again as he met the judge's eye. 'Sad,' said the witness, after a moment's reflection.

'Thank you, madam,' said O'Brien, and sat down abruptly.

Sophie was preparing to leave the witness box when the judge called her back. 'I think Mr Maitland also has some

177

questions for you,' he told her. 'Mr Maitland is Dr Colling-wood's counsel,' he explained.

'Oh, very well,' said the witness ungraciously. Any awe she might have originally felt at finding herself giving evidence seemed to have left her now.

Maitland got up slowly and stood looking at her for a long moment. That was a trick he had borrowed from Garfield, who so often used it in cross-examination; and indeed Antony's chameleon-like behaviour in the face of other people's mannerisms had got him into trouble more than once in the past. Now, however, Garfield was as unconscious of the mimicry as James Collingwood's counsel was. Only the judge was aware of it, and wondered what Maitland had in store for them now.

He started decorously enough. 'I will not detain you long, madam. My learned friend, Mr O'Brien, has covered most of the points with you that you had not seen fit to mention before.'

'I'm sure I don't know what you mean,' said the witness, bridling. At least, that was how Antony put it to himself, though he would have been the first to admit that he had never seen it done before.

'Your statement to the police missed out one or two essentials,' Maitland pointed out. 'I cannot believe that my honourable and learned friend for the prosecution was badly briefed,' he added courteously.

'I answered everything they asked me.'

'I see. Well, I have only one question for you, though it may lead to others. Was Mrs Johnstone the only person you saw on the first floor, the bedroom floor, that day?'

'I didn't see the doctor up there, if that's what you mean, but we know he went up to the nursery.'

'That, as I think you know, is not what I mean at all. Who took up the children's tea?'

'It wasn't my place to.'

'Who took it up?' He was frankly pressing her now, and the questions came quickly.

'It was Delia's place to do it.' She paused an instant and then added unwillingly, 'But she wasn't there that day.'

'Who took it up then?' asked Maitland again. 'I'm sure Miss Gatsby, with her hands full with two lively children, wouldn't be expected to come down to the kitchen to fetch it.'

'Too grand for that,' said Sophie sulkily. 'Not to be expected of her, that's what I was told. Well, I'm not above helping out when asked right,' she added, with a certain unexpected assumption of virtue.

'So you took it up that day? And I'm sure, being as conscientious as you are, you went up in good time.'

'Yes, I did.'

'Did you use the front or the back stairs?'

'The front. It's easier, when you're carrying a tray.'

'Can you give me an estimate of what the time would be?'

'Just before the half-hour.'

'Half past five?'

'That's right.'

He felt the first stirring of excitement. It was like drawing teeth, but he was pretty sure now that there was something there to uncover. 'You saw, or heard, something when you were crossing the landing on the first floor,' he asserted.

'Well, I –'

'Either you did or you didn't.'

That brought a toss of the head, perhaps she was remembering O'Brien's warning. In any event, he could almost hear her thinking, I was never one to cut off my nose to spite my face. 'Well then, I did,' she said.

'Saw something, or heard something?'

'Both, if you want to know. She must just have gone into her bedroom –'

'Mrs Johnstone?' he asked sharply.

'Who else?'

179

'You really must answer the question yes or no,' said Carruthers, leaning forward.

'Yes, my lord.' She was sulking again and did not continue until Maitland had prompted her. 'I thought she had just gone in because she called out in a questioning sort of way, "Jean!"'

'And did Mrs Lamb answer her?'

'Of course she didn't, she wasn't there.' Suddenly her reluctance left her, he thought she was feeling a sudden upsurge of power in knowing something of which all these people were ignorant. 'Mrs Lamb was standing at the other side of the landing, half hidden by what they call an *armoire*. I didn't let on as I'd seen her, I thought that might have made her feel awkward, seeing as she'd no right or reason to be over there.'

Garfield was on his feet, but had only just succeeded in catching the judge's eye. 'I am sorry, Mr Garfield, I must disallow your objection,' said Carruthers. 'When Mr Maitland is in this mood, there is nothing for it but to humour him.'

Maitland gave Garfield a look that was almost apologetic. The momentary excitement had died now, he was aware only of a great weariness. He wanted his client to go free, and Kate Johnstone too, of course, that went without saying. But he didn't like this business, he didn't like it at all, and even if he got the final admission he wanted it still wouldn't be anything like proof. He turned again to the witness. 'Where was Mrs Lamb standing in relation to Douglas Johnstone's bedroom?' he asked.

'She was just by it, only as if she had moved a little towards the *armoire* so that I wouldn't see her.'

'The position of Mr Johnstone's bedroom – ?'

'At the back of the house, on the left hand side of the landing.'

'Thank you, madam.' Maitland looked at the judge with

180

something that was very much like despair. 'No more questions for this witness, my lord,' he said.

None of his colleagues spoke to him as he sat down again, but to his utter surprise O'Brien laid a hand, briefly but sympathetically, on his arm.

II

The prosecution had still one more witness to call, Doctor John Trevelyan, in whose employ James Collingwood had been. It was obvious from the beginning that his sympathies were with the defence; he gave, unasked, what amounted to a character reference for Maitland's client, and earned a mild rebuke from the judge for offering an unsolicited opinion. But there was nothing much that he could do. There was a shortage in his morphine supply, he couldn't explain it because it was a drug he never used, and out of deference to his opinion he was pretty sure James Collingwood had never used it either. He talked a good deal about the amount of 'spillage' that might be regarded as normal, but the jury couldn't help but get the impression that it was his supply the murderer had used. In addition, he had to admit that he had told his assistant of his call to see Dougie Johnstone on the morning of his father's death; so that there was no need of a further visit in the afternoon, no need at all.

O'Brien's cross-examination was merely concerned to put as good a construction on these uncomfortable facts as was possible, but he seemed resigned now to the course that Maitland had determined and wished him good luck when he in turn got up to face the witness. By tacit consent, both men ignored the question of why the doctor had gone to the Johnstone house at all, when it was no longer his custom to attend the children. There might be an equally uncomfortable answer to that . . . the one that Collingwood had suggested to his counsel, for instance.

'Dr Trevelyan.' A sympathetic witness, no need for hectoring tactics here. 'You have told my honourable and learned friend, Mr Garfield, that the morphine was kept in a locked cupboard in your surgery. But the key was not put in a very imaginative hiding place, I think you will admit that.'

'I suppose that if anyone were looking for it, the middle drawer of my desk would be the first place they'd think of.'

'But you had, of course, no reason to think that anybody would look for the key?'

'No reason in the world.'

'All the same, I understand that you don't keep regular surgery hours. Most of your patients prefer to be visited at home.'

'That is quite correct.'

'So there must be many occasions when your office is empty?'

Dr Trevelyan smiled in a deprecating way, as though the question somehow embarrassed him. 'More often than not the room is empty,' he agreed.

'Do you think it is conceivable that someone from outside might come in?'

'I don't think my receptionist would see anyone unless they reported to her room.'

'Is Mrs Jean Lamb one of your patients?' That question came more abruptly, and the witness looked anxiously at Counsel for the Prosecution.

'Is that a proper question for me to answer?' he enquired.

The judge spoke before Garfield could make either reply or protest. 'I think, Dr Trevelyan, that in the circumstances you may answer,' he said.

'Very well then.' He wasn't happy about it, but he answered without hesitation. 'Mrs Lamb is among my patients.'

'Perhaps also among your personal friends?'

'That is true. She and her husband both.'

'Now, Doctor, if morphine was indeed missing from your supply, you have no idea when it might have been taken?'

182

'No idea at all.'

'Suppose we postulate a period of, say, two weeks before Douglas Johnstone's death. Will you cast your mind back to that time?'

The doctor frowned over that. Perhaps he found it difficult to comply, but it did seem that he was taking the question seriously. 'I'm not quite sure what you want to know,' he said, at last.

'Could anything unusual have happened during that period, anything at all?'

'I don't recall anything of the sort.'

'Wait a bit!' Maitland was absorbed in his witness, but insensibly his manner had become a little less formal. 'I want you to think very carefully, Doctor. What I have in mind is something that might have been the occasion of an unauthorised visit to your surgery.'

'I – ' He shook his head in a bewildered way. There was an agonising pause, during which Maitland had time to think of the likely fruits of failure, before the witness spoke again. 'I haven't thought about it before,' he said, 'but there was the telephone call. Though I don't see what that could have had to do with it.'

Maitland was suddenly very still. O'Brien, beside him, had the impression that he was holding his breath, perhaps afraid to break the silence that had developed. 'The telephone call?' he said at last very softly, and made the words a question.

'It was nothing really, the sort of thing that happens nowadays.'

'Please explain, Doctor.'

'A hoax,' said Dr Trevelyan, indignant all over again in remembering the episode. 'A call came in – when I questioned my receptionist later she said it was a woman's voice – asking me to visit a very old patient of mine immediately, as she had had a heart attack. When I got to her house I found her hale and hearty, and just starting her tea.'

'That was at teatime, then.'

'I suppose the call came in at half past three. But my patient doesn't live very near, it would take me quite half an hour to reach her house with the traffic as it is today.'

'And half an hour to return?' Maitland sounded reflective. 'So you were gone for a full hour.'

'A little more than that, because she insisted that I take a cup of tea with her. I was a little worried about that, because –'

'Because what, Doctor?'

'This can't concern this unfortunate business, but I suppose I must answer.' Dr Trevelyan's tone was one of almost humorous resignation. 'My wife was expecting me, because we had a visitor coming for tea and she wanted me to be there.'

The strain in Maitland's voice was very evident now; it seemed as though he could hardly bear to break the silence. 'Who was that visitor?' he said, but not until the atmosphere in the courtroom had become almost intolerable.

Again the doctor looked round, but this time he didn't wait for the judge's ruling. 'The lady you mentioned before,' he said. 'Mrs Jean Lamb.'

'And when you got home did you in fact find that she had visited Mrs Trevelyan that afternoon?'

'They were still sitting together. Of course my wife understood –'

'Thank you, Doctor. You have remembered so much, perhaps I might ask you to put your mind to another, smaller, problem. There is a door, is there not, between your house and the annex that has been built on to hold the surgeries?'

'Two doors, to be exact, one on each floor of the annex.'

'Are these doors kept locked?'

'There is no need. We lock them at night, but that is probably an unnecessary precaution. During the day . . . they are there for our convenience, and it seems more convenient to leave them open.'

'Thank you, Doctor,' said Maitland again. He looked all round the court before he seated himself, as though trying to judge the effect of what had passed. 'I have no more questions,' he said then, and watched without surprise as Garfield got up to re-examine.

As soon as Counsel for the Prosecution had finished pouring ridicule on the recent cross-examination, the judge adjourned for the luncheon recess. Vera was not in court today, somewhat to Maitland's relief, and he was pretty sure that Meg was not among the spectators either. There was, therefore, a little discussion among the various members of the defence team, but finally Antony and Kevin set out alone for Astroff's.

By common consent they went into the bar first. 'I suppose you realise you've burnt your boats,' said O'Brien, after their drinks had been served and the waiter had vanished again. 'If the verdict goes against us now –'

'I realise that all right.' Maitland was making a valiant attempt at a casual tone. 'A rather shabby trick, attacking an innocent woman. That's what they'll say.'

'Well, I got you into it; and there have been times,' O'Brien admitted, 'when I've regretted it. But you've certainly done your best.'

Nothing, had he but known it, could have been better calculated to rouse Maitland to anger. Perhaps that would have been a good thing, shaking off his present apathy, but before he could make any response there was an interruption. A man stopped by their table and a voice he felt he ought to recognise said huskily, 'I've got to talk to you, gentlemen.'

He looked up and saw it was Ernest Lamb.

III

Maitland was braced for squalls, and he was pretty sure that O'Brien read the signs the same way. He hadn't noticed Lamb among the spectators that morning, but no doubt he had been there, and after what had been said . . . So he was all the more surprised when Lamb, instead of starting on an angry tirade, pulled out a chair and seated himself, saying only as an afterthought, 'Do you mind if I sit down?'

O'Brien recovered his composure, or at least his tongue, before his colleague did. 'I really don't think there's anything we can usefully say to each other,' he said.

Ernest Lamb was mopping his brow. 'I only wish you were right.' And Maitland realised as he spoke that this was not merely anger at the insinuations that had been made in court; the man was in a state of mental anguish, not wanting to speak, and yet impelled by some inner force to do so.

'Just take your time, Mr Lamb,' he suggested. 'We don't reconvene until two o'clock.'

'What I have to say won't take that long.' He looked at O'Brien and then back at Maitland again, perhaps sensing in the latter a greater understanding of his needs. 'You've done a good job of proving that Jean could have killed Douglas,' he said. His voice was tinged with bitterness, but at the same time, oddly, there seemed to be no rancour behind the remark.

'We may have proved opportunity, but that isn't the same thing as a Not Guilty verdict for our clients, you know.' Maitland might almost have been reassuring him.

'That's why I'm here,' said Lamb, and fell silent again.

After a while Maitland spoke gently, though he was well enough aware that there was no way of softening the impact of his words. 'We know she had the opportunity, though whether she had the means is still problematical. And *I*

186

know – though this is one of the insubstantial things that are difficult to prove – that *you* had a motive.'

'That's why I'm here,' said Lamb again. 'It's all my fault,' he went on still in the same anguished tone. 'I shouldn't have talked so much about how I'd like to dissolve the partnership, like to be in full control. You see there was an opportunity of making really big money – '

'But Mrs Lamb was . . . interested, shall we say?'

'Oh, more than that.' Suddenly the words were pouring out of him. 'She questioned me endlessly about what we could do about it. Only there really wasn't anything. Douglas wasn't the easiest man to get on with, but I'd no cause of complaint against him, and with a deal like that in the offing naturally he wouldn't want to step down.'

'I see your dilemma. So what did you do about it?'

'Nothing at all; I swear to you!'

'But now you think that Mrs Lamb was interested enough to take some action on her own?' He was treading warily, but Ernest Lamb had reached a stage where speech was as essential to him as breathing.

'Think? I'm sure of it! Why else do you think I'm here? I couldn't believe it, even yesterday evening, and I asked her . . . I thought then that her manner was . . . that she wasn't being quite open with me, but perhaps she was just angry with me for thinking any such thing. We've had our ups and downs, but she's been a good wife to me. Mr Maitland. But I'm fond of Kate, and I swear to you that if I'd known what had happened – '

'You say your wife denied that she had taken any action to realise your ambitions.'

'Yes, she did, and I'm sure if I asked her again she would say the same thing. But I stayed behind after she left for court this morning, and I made a search of her things. And I found a hypodermic – we never had any use for such a thing – and these ampoules with it. There's an empty one in the syringe, but the others . . . Oh God!'

187

Maitland and O'Brien exchanged glances. 'And you think – ?' said Maitland tentatively, turning back to Ernest Lamb again.

'What could I think but that she had done it? I was frantic,' said Lamb, and neither of his hearers doubted for a moment the truth of what he said. 'And then when I got to court in time for your cross-examination of the parlourmaid . . . I knew I had to talk to you, I didn't see any way out.'

'And we're grateful to you.' Maitland's voice was formal, this was no time for encouraging emotionalism. O'Brien, more practically, was signalling the waiter, and ordered without reference to the newcomer a double Black Label. 'We have to talk about this, Maitland,' he said, when the drink had been brought and Lamb was clutching at it like a lifeline. 'What's the best way to deal with the situation?'

'It depends a good deal on Mr Lamb.' The gentleman referred to was drinking the whisky as if he were thirsty. 'Are you willing to repeat what you've told us to the Counsel for the Prosecution?' Maitland enquired.

'I know that I must.' There was no resolution in Lamb's tone, he sounded a broken man. 'You see, she'd never . . . she'd never . . . if she was sane . . . I can't let her go on and perhaps hurt somebody else. But I have to make it clear to everybody that I was to blame.'

'I take it then – '

'Yes . . . yes . . . yes!'

They let him finish his drink in peace, but the idea of food obviously revolted him. Presently he seemed to sink into a sort of stupor, and for want of any better idea the two barristers continued their conversation in a low tone. There was obviously no question of turning this new witness adrift by himself in his present state of mind. 'As soon as we get back to court, we'll ask for a consultation with Carruthers in chambers,' said O'Brien. 'With Garfield present, of course. I don't think after that there'll be any difficulty if we ask for a recess until the police have had time to make some further enquiries.'

'Sykes always says,' Maitland told him, and he sounded very subdued, 'that once you know where to look there's always evidence to be found. And in this case – ' He broke off there, because it suddenly seemed impossible to say anything more. He had been very sure, or he wouldn't have embarked on the dangerous course he had taken; but now the realisation that, after all, he might have been wrong hit him suddenly. It might have been that that was making him feel so sick, or it might have been Ernest Lamb's predicament, or perhaps his own part in the proceedings.

'In this case you were right all along the line,' O'Brien was saying handsomely. 'But do you agree with the course I've outlined? It seems to me the only thing to be done.'

'I a-agree, all r-right,' said Maitland, the stammer that usually plagued him only when he was angry becoming suddenly very obvious. He realised the inevitability of the events he had set in train, but that didn't make him like them any better. 'I think I'd b-better have another d-drink before we make a m-move,' he added. 'I seem to need something to pull me together as much as our friend here does.'

That was a course with which O'Brien, more sensitive to his colleague's needs than some people would have given him credit for, heartily agreed. Afterwards, not without some difficulties, not without some arguments from Garfield, they carried out the programme he had outlined. But Garfield, whatever faults he might have in Maitland's eyes, was a man with a strong sense of justice, and in the end they got their way.

The recess was granted, but neither of them felt in much of a mood for rejoicing. Their instructing solicitors were despatched to break the good news to their clients.

189

TUESDAY, after the verdict

That Tuesday afternoon Antony came home early from court, and was surprised to find Sir Nicholas and Vera, as well as Roger and Meg, having tea with Jenny. 'Where the carcase is, there shall the eagles be gathered together,' he commented, not very politely, as he crossed the room.

'We wanted to know exactly how things turned out, darling,' Meg explained.

Since the subject had been discussed exhaustively during the weekend, Antony found this unreasonable. 'It was a foregone conclusion,' he protested.

'Not as foregone as all that,' said Roger.

'Once the woman in the shop identified Jean Lamb as one of her customers, the police were certain it was she who sent the chocolates here. Added to everything else . . . the morphine was the real clincher, you know.'

'I suppose it was,'

'Poor Mr Lamb,' said Jenny.

'But there is something you don't know,' Antony admitted. 'Jean has confessed, so you see – '

That brought a little buzz of conversation into which Sir Nicholas's voice broke languidly. 'I suppose you are going to tell me, Antony, that right has triumphed once more.' He sounded bored, but Maitland knew better than to take that at face value.

'Nothing quite so smug, I hope,' he said.

'I wonder if you realise what a lucky escape you've had,' his uncle went on meditatively. 'If Lamb hadn't turned up when he did, with a crucial piece of evidence – '

'My name would be mud. I know that,' said Maitland crudely. Sir Nicholas, who affected an extreme aversion to slang, closed his eyes and appeared to fall into swoon. Ignoring him, Antony added in a more sober way, returning to what he had said a moment before, 'I'm not feeling smug about it at all, as a matter of fact.'

Jenny, as perhaps were some of the others, was perfectly well aware of that fact. She knew his reactions to the end of a case only too well. 'I wonder why she did it,' she said. 'Do you suppose she's really mad?'

'Her unfortunate husband obviously thinks so. No, I think she genuinely expected his approval of what she had done, and when she found he was sufficiently shaken by it to give her away nothing seemed to matter any more.'

Vera had a question there. 'D'you really think he didn't know?' she asked.

'If you had talked to him . . . I really think he didn't know,' Antony assured her.

'But you haven't told us yet what happened in court today,' said Jenny, who liked to get things straight.

'Garfield did his stuff, offered no more evidence, asked for the case to be dismissed. So Carruthers directed the jury to return a verdict of Not Guilty, and that was that. When the news of Jean Lamb's arrest gets about everybody will know the verdict was the right one, so there's nothing to stop my client and his lady love from living happily ever after.'

'Poor Mr Lamb,' sighed Jenny again. And then, more hopefully, 'Do you think they will?'

'I expect so. Do you know,' he asked returning to a point of more interest to him, 'Kate still can't remember leaving Jean alone on the first floor that day. She remembers going up to the nursery all right, but not that she left Jean while she did so.'

'Her visit was so ordinary, she took it for granted. But I think Kate must have a very nice nature,' said Jenny, always

191

happiest to see the good in people, 'never even to have suspected.'

'Still don't see,' said Vera, 'how Ernest Lamb could live with her all those years, and never realise what sort of a woman she was.'

'Evidently a gentleman of very little perception,' said Sir Nicholas thoughtfully. At some time during the foregoing exchange, he seemed to have revived from his swoon.

'I don't agree with you there, Uncle Nick.' Antony, too, was thinking it out. 'Everyone who knew her was unanimous in saying what a nice person she was; and when I saw her in court, even when I realised what she was trying to do to Kate ... well it was hard to believe, that's all.'

'A sort of Lady Macbeth,' said Meg in her deepest voice. 'I could have told you what she was like.'

'Then why the – why didn't you?' Antony demanded.

'You'd have said it was good theatre, but not real life,' said Meg. And when he thought about it afterwards he realised that perhaps there was some truth in that after all.